St. Augustine, Florida

A *Jamaican* LADY

ROBERT PHILLIP JONES AND VENASA TASHANA WALKER

outskirts
press

A Jamaican Lady
Chasing the American Dream From Jamaica to St. Augustine, Florida
All Rights Reserved.
Copyright © 2022 Robert Phillip Jones and Venasa Tashana Walker
v2.0

This is a work of fiction. Names, characters, businesses, places, events, locales, and incidents are either the products of the author's imagination or used in a fictitious manner. Any resemblance to actual persons, living or dead, or actual events is purely coincidental.

The opinions expressed in this manuscript are solely the opinions of the author and do not represent the opinions or thoughts of the publisher. The author has represented and warranted full ownership and/or legal right to publish all the materials in this book.

This book may not be reproduced, transmitted, or stored in whole or in part by any means, including graphic, electronic, or mechanical without the express written consent of the publisher except in the case of brief quotations embodied in critical articles and reviews.

Outskirts Press, Inc.
http://www.outskirtspress.com

ISBN: 978-1-9772-5847-2

Cover Photo © 2022 www.gettyimages.com. All rights reserved - used with permission.

Outskirts Press and the "OP" logo are trademarks belonging to Outskirts Press, Inc.

PRINTED IN THE UNITED STATES OF AMERICA

Thank You

A very special thanks to Steve 'Borny' Bornhoft for the hours he spent editing 'A Jamaican Lady.' We do not know how many red pencils he used to make a good story better, but his benevolence is appreciated very much.

Steve Bornhoft is a special person in every sense of the word. Honesty in all that he does is how he is known. Genuine interest in the people he meets, and the professional kindness toward the stories they tell, is his mantra.

Thank you, young warrior.

Bob Jones & Venasa Walker

ROBERT PHILLIP JONES AND
VENASA TASHANA WALKER
co-authors

A JAMAICAN LADY ©

Chapter One

TIANA BENNETT'S TRIP TO ST. MARY PARISH IN JAMAICA — IT WAS A MISSION, REALLY — BEGAN IN ST. AUGUSTINE, FLORIDA. She went seeking to learn more about her ancestors dating to her seven-great grandfather. She had anecdotal information and a few records that indicated he fought as a Black British soldier during America's War of Independence.

She wanted more.

The Boeing-737 landed smoothly at a crowded Norman Manley International Airport in Kingston. She retrieved her luggage from the carousel and turned to see a smiling Grandpa Bennett waiting outside the security area to take her to his home. They caught up during the two-hour drive from Kingston to the Bennett house three miles from Oracabessa. She hoped there was phone service at the house. She wanted to call Phillip to tell him she had arrived safely.

Dogs began barking the moment Tiana stepped out of her grandfather's car. Among them was Brownie, who was just a noisy mongrel puppy when Tiana and her daughter Chandice migrated to St. Augustine seven years earlier. Brownie came from a litter of pups that her mama birthed under the cellar of the house. Everybody in the community had dogs.

When Grandpa began feeding Brownie table scraps, she became territorial. Anyone who wanted to enter the Bennett yard had to call from the gate because Brownie would growl and bark at them.

"Brownie, Brownie," Tiana said.

The dog stopped barking and came to Tiana, wagging her tail at the sight of someone she loved. Well trained, Brownie, did not jump on Tiana, and she was glad for that. The dog had grown to 40 pounds in her absence. Brownie followed her up the front steps, but stopped and sat down when the front door opened.

Gramma stood in the doorway, smiling and wearing a long house dress. She had her favorite black, green and yellow apron tied around her waist and a multi-colored cloth tied around her hair. Tiana told her she did not look like she had aged a bit. She grabbed Tiana with her still strong arms and then put her luggage away. Tiana and her grandparents walked around the outside of the house. The front-yard garden was full of corn, tomatoes, okra, cabbage, gunja and peas. Gramma Bennett made the best okra and tomato dish around.

All the fruit trees in the backyard were healthy. The avocado tree she planted when she lived there as a child had doubled in size. They stood under the shade of a large ackee tree and reminisced until it was time for the evening meal.

After supper they gathered in the living room and talked and laughed and cried some more. Tiana asked her grandmother if she remembered the Baptist missionaries who came once a year from Canada to check the teeth of all the kids in the neighborhood, teach hygiene and do their missionary work. Gramma said she remembered them well and recalled hearing stories about white plantation owners criticizing the Baptist missionaries over their views on slavery.

White slave owners said the missionaries were preaching freedom for slaves, a prospect that would wreck the economy of the island. Sugar plantation owners had little concern for the welfare of the enslaved. Slaves were chattel.

It was midnight when Tiana walked to the bedroom to sleep in the same bed she slept in as a child. Cares and anxiety slipped away as she put her nightgown on. They disappeared when her head touched the pillow.

Tiana tossed back her grandmother's beloved comforter as soon as the rooster crowed. She yawned, stretched her arms high in the air and sat up on the edge of the bed. She smiled at the framed Latin words over the headboard next to the horseshoe. They had been there for decades: "Libera nos a malo." Deliver us from evil.

Tiana remembered that when she was growing up, both adults and children went to the river on Saturdays to get water that they transported in five-gallon buckets. Sometimes they walked on the donkey trails, but mostly they took a dreaded path in the woods that was laced with loose rocks and uneven ground that threatened to trip her. Tiana was young and could carry only a one-gallon bucket, but was sat-isfied that she was doing her part.

Living with her grandparents meant that she was expected to complete her chores before she did anything else.

She recalled how everybody in the neighborhood went into the forest to gather firewood. When they had enough, they washed their hands on leaves that were still wet with dew. On the way home, they picked avo-cados and tangerines from trees they passed. After church, the kids enjoyed ice cream, played cricket, a game played with rings called stuck, football and hide-and-seek for hours while the adults visited on the veranda.

The pit latrine was nearby, dry, and clean. It would be years before people could afford flush toilets. The community was safe when it won in-dependence from British colonial rule in 1962. There was no need to lock the doors, or even own a lock. That is not the case in 2022.

"Yuh getting up now Auntie fi Gramma's breakfast?" nine-year-old Aleiya asked, poking her head through the bedroom door.

"Mi soon come. Ali how yuh duh to-day? Ready fi wi trip by di bay."

"Yes Auntie," Aleiya responded, smiling.

"Aleiya, do you know what your name means?"

"No, Auntie."

"It is so true for you," she said. "Aleiya means strong, happy, and graceful. I found it on the Internet. It is perfect."

"I like that," Aleiya said as she skipped through the beads hanging from the door and went to the kitchen to help her grandmother.

The first iteration of the Bennett house was built in 1910 with dirt and stone and was later made larger with trees harvested from the forest. Grandpa gathered scraps from construction jobs and purchased wood from the lumber yard when he could. The house had a zinc roof, like most houses in Jamaica, because zinc lasts 80 years or so. Many times, people would build just two rooms for starters and add rooms later when money and supplies were available.

There was no electricity in the early years, but after Independence Day progress was made. The Bennetts used small tanks of propane gas for cooking when there was company, but otherwise cooked on the wood stove. Water was always available from the river a quarter of a mile down the hill. Fetching it was a ritual.

Tiana heated a pot of water on the stove and had a quick bath. She wrapped her trim body in the towel her grandmother had laid out. She patted her dreadlocks dry, pulled up her khaki shorts and buttoned her sheer yellow, cotton blouse. Her mahogany brown eyes glanced in the mirror at the 5-foot, 6-inch woman she had become. She was fit and weighed 110 pounds.

Tiana noticed a strand of gray in her dreadlocks. She smiled and stepped into her flat sneakers. She walked to a window overlooking the backyard and saw the "baby tree" where her mother had buried her placenta and umbilical cord after Tiana was born. Tiana buried the placenta and cord from Chandice's birth under the same ackee tree.

Tiana told Chandice about that ritual for the first time when she was six years old. Chandice told her mother it is something she will consider when she becomes a mother. Tiana was pleased the ackee tree was healthy. She felt spiritual vibes that she attributed to the tree.

The aroma wafting from the kitchen was irresistible. It reminded her of school days when Gramma always fixed a big breakfast. Tiana was ready

to enjoy ackee, saltfish, roasted bread-
fruit and chocolate tea. As she came
through the door, she chuckled at two
wooden placards Grandpa had made
and hung on the wall. "De olda de
moon, de brighter it shines," read one.
On the other was the Jamaican rule:

When you come here-
What you do here-
What you see here-
What you hear here-
When you leave here-
Let it stay here-
or don't come back here.

When she saw ackee on her plate,
Tiana smacked her lips. It is a taste she
savors even though when she was 11,
she ate unripened ackee and was so
sick she stayed in bed for three days.

In high school, she learned the sci-
entific name of ackee is *Blighia sapida*
and that it was named for the infamous

Captain Bligh of the *HMS Bounty*. Tiana wasn't taught much about Captain Bligh in school, but became familiar with his legend by watching *Mutiny on the Bounty* starring Marlon Brando as Lieutenant Christian Fletcher and Trevor Howard as Captain William Bligh. She has watched this classic movie at least five times.

Grandpa Bennett washed his hands outside, took his boots off, and walked into the kitchen. He wore the same long-sleeve plaid shirt he has worn for years. He wore a tattered apron over his tailor-made pants while he prepared the saltfish and fed the goats, chickens and two dozen rabbits that he received from a United Nations grant program. He was ready for breakfast. He laid his apron on the back porch table. Tiana gave him a big hug, and he cheerfully returned it.

Grandpa stood 6-3, and towered over Tiana. He tucked his dreadlocks inside his gold and green colored tam. He trimmed his graying beard and mustache twice a week. He was broad-shouldered, strong, and full of energy. At 74, he carried his 220 pounds with ease.

He was an artisanal fisherman, and Tiana hoped Grandpa would take her fishing with him during her visit. She knew how to bait, set, and pull the small fish traps he used in 90 feet of water to catch parrotfish. She appreciated him and other small-scale fishermen who kept artisanal fishing alive in St. Mary Parish.

He knew his chances were slim, but Grandpa Bennett was investigating whether he might supplement his income by harvesting Jamaica sea moss, a much sought-after superfood. It contains 92 of the 102 minerals required by human bodies. Unfortunately for him, most government funds go to corporations with enough capital to construct shoreside multi-million-dollar infrastructure.

The wild harvest of myriad species of fish in the world is discouraged. Aquaculture is popular with politicians. Vast amounts of money have been invested to create meatless meat products. Grandpa told Gramma, "I hate to think what a 'make-believe' yellowtail snapper would taste like."

Jamaica's territorial sea extends 12 nautical miles from shore. It has a contiguous zone of 24 miles and continental shelf authority of 200 nautical miles. Grandpa Bennett fishes in the territorial sea. Marine law enforcement constables inspect his catch when he returns to land. He and his fellow fishermen complain about the lack of enforcement in various fisheries, but they don't have the political power to change the laws or enforcement priorities.

Other nations seeking access to Jamaican waters would use industrial fishing gear. Their factory ships might easily overwhelm the resources that artisanal fishermen have relied upon for generations. Precisely that scenario has played out in other parts of the world.

Tiana glanced at the scar on Grandpa's neck and remembered how he got it. He had been injured during a robbery at the Oracabessa fish market six months ago. Newspaper accounts described how two robbers targeted the fish market in broad daylight. Police reports said both men were high and intoxicated.

Grandpa Bennett was counting his pay when the robbery started. He had just delivered 30 pounds of fresh parrotfish to a wholesale buyer. The shorter and stockier of the two robbers tried to grab the money from Bennett's hand, but Grandpa was much stronger. He practically crushed the robber's hand, then kicked him ferociously in the groin, taking him out of the fray. He would be in severe pain for at least a week.

The taller, uglier robber standing by the cash register turned toward Grandpa and swore at him with words that would shock a sailor. Flailing away with a hatchet he pulled from his belt, he grazed Grandpa as he backed away from his assailant with his arms at his sides. Grandpa tripped over a fish box and fell to the floor. He would have been slashed to pieces except another fishermen knocked the robber to the floor with one powerful swing of his fish gaff. Fishermen quickly bound the hands and feet of the two robbers and kept them there moaning and groaning and cussing until the Constabulary Force arrived.

A tourist trained in first aid stepped forward and tied a piece of cloth around Grandpa's neck. She kept pressure on the wound with her hand until she and Grandpa arrived at the hospital. The doctor quickly put 12 stiches in his neck to stop the bleeding. An hour later, a friend drove Grandpa home. Jamaicans avoid staying overnight in any hospital if possible.

"How you feeling, Grampa," Tiana asked.

"Pretty gud fi mi age, me a elder now," he said chuckling.

"What's an elder? I have known elders at 50 and young bucks at 80," she replied.

"I want you to bring that 80-year-old-young-buck to this house right away," he said with a devilish grin . "Mi wan di secret mi can be a young-buck at 74."

Grandpa laughed and Tiana rolled her eyes, slightly shook her head and smiled.

Chapter Two

AFTER A SCRUMPTIOUS BREAKFAST, TIANA TOOK HER SECOND CUP OF CHOCOLATE TEA TO THE VERANDA. It was the main gathering place for neighbors in the evening. She sat in one of the old rocking chairs arranged across the highly polished red floor. The veranda, furniture and entire scene looked the same as it did when she lived there as a child.

The sun was up. Clouds moved gently to the east in unison against a bright blue Jamaican sky. The temperature was 75 degrees and was expected to reach 90 by mid-afternoon. It was going to be another beautiful day in paradise, one that would resemble the cover of a tourist brochure.

Fatta, the eldest of the Bennett dogs, waddled towards Tiana and took his place on the blanket in the corner of the veranda. Fatta was fat from birth. That made naming him simple. He was a happy mongrel that was loved by everyone in the neighborhood. He was 15 years old. His time was approaching. He showed his age.

Tiana had an appointment in Kingston at the Jamaica historical Foundation. She was searching for records about Wilbert Bennett, her seven-great grandfather. She had been told that he was a British soldier who migrated to Jamaica from St. Augustine after the American War of Independence.

She reviewed letters and diaries about the heroic battles of British Admiral Lord George Brydges Rodney, especially his defeat of the French fleet when it attempted to invade Jamaica in 1782.

She would tell Phillip when she returned to St. Augustine that it was all she could do to keep from going down all the 'rabbit holes' that the archives presented to her. Little of what she was learning had been taught to her in school. She will tell Phillip that it should have been.

Lord Rodney had a colorful history. Prior to his being called back to England to become admiral of the fleet, he was hiding in Paris from his creditors for three years. He had a gambling problem.

Tiana found a clipping that was published after Lord Rodney's victory over the French at New York and again at the battle of the Saints.

The clipping read …

In September 1780, leaving half of his fleet in West Indian waters, Rodney sailed to New York and foiled George Washington's designs for a Franco-American land-and-sea assault on the city. Returning to the Caribbean in

February 1781, Rodney captured the Dutch islands of St. Eustatius and St. Martin and confiscated huge stocks belonging to British merchants trading illegally with American Revolutionists, thereby crippling a contraband trade on which the Americans depended. For the rest of his life, he engaged in lawsuits with British merchants over this action.

After the murder of George Floyd in Minneapolis, Minnesota, and the growth of the Black Lives Matter movement across the world, there were calls made for the removal of statues honoring imperialists and Lord Rodney's statue was one that was mentioned.

From the *Jamaica Gleaner* ....

The *Gleaner* reported Jamaica's Culture Minister Olivia Grange has opened the door for discussion on removing statues of colonial-era icons from public spaces. The minister said that the Holness administration was satisfied that the emerging discourse was necessary to fully confront the inequities and injustices of the past that are impacting modern life.

"The Government understands that peaceful protests, robust public debate, and even the changing of symbols are part of a process that every generation must go through in defining ourselves as a race and a nation of people," Grange told *The Gleaner*.

Tiana also found a copy of a letter notifying British soldiers and loyalists that they could migrate to Jamaica as well as the Bahamas or Canada. Tiana believes her seven-great grandfather accepted Colonel Deveaux's offer authorizing any volunteers who joined him in the retaking the Bahamas to migrate to Jamaica.

A February 1783 letter from Colonel Deveaux to the British commander Sir Guy Carleton proposed an expedition to free the Bahamas from the Spanish so that British loyalists leaving America would have another safe haven.

Colonel Deveaux and his volunteers removed the Spanish presence not knowing that a peace treaty between England and Spain had returned the Bahamas to the British. The Bahamas remained part of the British Empire until July 10, 1973.

Tiana spent 300 Jamaican dollars on phone cards at the Kingston airport in case she had to call her boss. She worked for the St. Johns County Clerk of the Court and had submitted her department's budget request before she left for Jamaica. She was confident that the request was in order, but there might be a need to clarify an item or two.

The Digicel telephone company salesman told her she would always have service where she was going to be staying. She had her doubts.

She was surprised when her phone vibrated.

She saw the caller's name and smiled.

"Hello, Phillip."

"Good morning, young lady. Glad you had a safe trip. Are you working on your project?"

"Not today," Tiana said. "I'm taking Aleiya on a sightseeing trip to Oracabessa by Sea. We're acting like tourists. We are going for a boat ride in the bay after we visit the waterfall if the weather stays good. I am going to Kingston tomorrow for next appointment at the Jamaica Historical Foundation. I expect to find the names of British loyalists who migrated and settled here from St. Augustine in 1784."

"It's a long shot but surely worth a

try." Phillip said. "I'm at the St. Augustine Historical Society looking at *East Florida Newspapers* on microfilm. Jamaican citations are rare."

There was a momentary pause in the conversation.

"How are you really getting along, Phillip?" Tiana said. "It's been almost a year since Louisa died. Everyone knows how tough losing her is for you."

"I sit in my recliner in the Florida room every morning looking at the activity on Matanzas Bay, St. Augustine's skyline and the fort. The crepe myrtle tree George Lewes planted for Louisa bloomed profusely in only six weeks. Every day a female redbird sits in the branches and then flies to the feeder so I can watch her eat sunflower seeds," he said. "It usually happens at the same time I'm thinking about Louisa. I have to believe she visits to tell me hello. I can almost hear her saying, with a smile on her face, 'Phillip, Phillip, are you behaving yourself?' and then she says, 'I love you.'"

"Oh, Phillip," Tiana said. "What a blessing. How sweet that must feel."

"While I am sitting there, I also think about the relationship we have and how unusual it might seem to people who knew Louisa. I hope my family understands we are all on the right paths in our journey of life. My path is already decided. You and all of Louisa's caregivers are on my path and part of my life," he said. "Thanks be to God.

"One day at a time Tiana. Friends are the best medicine I have felt since losing Louisa. Everyone I know has lost someone they love. They know my feelings. I know theirs."

"Yes, that's a special kind of medicine for sure. Love from family and friends and the grace of God is where you are," Tiana said. "Your eyes are a getting brighter and your step a little lighter each day. Working on our ancestral history is good medicine for both of us."

"Yes, it is," he said. " I miss you. I will be glad when you return."

"Miss you, too," she said with kindness in her voice. "I will let you know when I will be home."

"Be well and be safe," Phillip said.

Phillip looked at the 'Quote of the Day' on his cellphone. Today's, attributed to Epicurus, was appropriate.

"Of all the means which wisdom acquires to ensure happiness throughout the whole of life, by far the most important is friendship."

Phillip Usina is a 75-year-old brick mason and plasterer. His Minorcan heritage in Saint Augustine is legendary. Louisa, his loving wife of 49 years, was also born in Saint Augustine. Their ancestors were indentured servants from the island of Minorca in the Balearic Islands when they were young. They sailed from Minorca to St. Augustine in 1768. The Usina and Oliveros families have been continuous residents of St. Augustine since they fled Andrew Turnbull's indigo plantation in 1777.

Phillip quit working at large construction sites on his 70th birthday. He no longer climbs up and down multistory scaffolds. He has tinnitus in his left elbow from lifting thousands of concrete blocks, plastering and troweling cement for the last 50 years. For the past five years, he has done restoration work at the Ponce de Leon Hotel and other historical buildings.

He was the masonry man of choice when historically accurate brickwork was needed. He was a master plasterer and could make any wall or ceiling as slick as a cue ball. He restored damaged plaster artwork around gigantic chandeliers originally created by European artisans brought to St. Augustine by Henry Flagler.

Phillip's coquina masonry work was exquisite. He and masonry friends in the Masters and Pacetti clans knew all the tricks of the trade to create perfect coquina blocks. Phillip made the exact sizes and shapes according to specifications. He used the same handmade tools his great-grandfather used when he made coquina blocks from the quarry on Anastasia Island.

Philip loved fishing. Louisa said he loved fishing better than the masonry trade. He knew every creek in St. Johns County. He knew the best time and best tides to catch trout, redfish, sheepshead, and whiting. He always carried his cast net with him in case he saw a mullet jump.

He learned about the importance of marshes and wetlands at an early age. He listened to old fishermen on P.J. Manucy's dock cuss the government whenever developers received a permit to fill in a marsh with dirt. He abhorred the destruction of marshes. He knew marshes were critical to sustaining fish in the rivers of St. Johns County.

When marshes and wetlands are dredged and filled, they are lost forever as a food producing source, storm surge protector and water filter. Millions and millions of marine critters cannot exist without the marshes.

Phillip was astute in working through the maze of Ancestry.com. He traced his Usina ancestors back to 1768 with church and government documents and from reading all the books written about the Minorcans that he could find. His Usina ancestors migrated to St. Augustine as indentured servants. They signed contracts to work at Dr. Andrew Turnbull's indigo plantation in New Smyrna for up to nine years.

Things fell apart at the plantation. The Minorcans escaped New Smyrna in 1777 and walked to St. Augustine. Phillip tells anyone who will listen that the first freedom march in America was by the Minorcans."

Phillip recently completed 25 years of sobriety.

Phillip's friendship with Tiana began the first evening she arrived at his home as Louisa's caregiver. She came to the Usina home on Avista Circle in the evenings after working all day for the Clerk of the County Court.

Phillip, Louisa, and Tiana spent every evening talking about what was going on that day and making each other laugh. No subject was off limits. Phillip and Louisa discovered Tiana was an Jamaican immigrant. She was a single mom working two jobs to provide for herself and her daughter. She migrated to St. Augustine in 2015 and moved in with her mother. She became a nighttime caregiver in 2016 and worked for her uncle at his Jamaican restaurant during the day.

She only works two nights a week now as a caregiver and hopes to quit that job in 2023. Tiana knew before she arrived that she would not be free until she achieved economic freedom. Louisa was impressed with Tiana's energy, work ethic and the sing-song of her delightful Jamaican accent. Phillip and Louisa were glad Tiana applied for U.S. citizenship.

Tiana and Phillip discussed current and historical politics in America and Jamaica. They agreed there were good people in both countries, but there were people in government interested only in power, prestige and possessions. Such people are found all over the world in all governments. They are not worth "the powder to blow them to hell," as the saying goes.

Tiana studied the 100 questions in a study guide in preparation for her citizenship examination. Only six questions are asked and if you miss one, you fail. She studied hard and answered all six questions correctly.

Phillip and Louisa were immensely proud of Tiana's accomplishment. She became a citizen of the United States of America in the manner our Constitution requires. There would have been a celebration in Jacksonville had it not been for pandemic protocols. When she came to the Usina house the next evening, Louisa and Phillip had a gift and special supper for the new citizen. Tiana had reached for the American Dream. She got a big part of it.

Phillip and Tiana's friendship developed steadily during the two years she was Louisa's caregiver. The depth of the friendship increased. They enjoyed each other's company even though Phillip was 75 with two children and five grandchildren and Tiana was 40 with one grown daughter. They felt relaxed when they talked each night after Louisa was in bed. They were doing everything possible to make Louisa comfortable and pain-free during the final phase of her journey.

Tiana was in the bedroom with Louisa every night and Phillip was in his office on the computer. One evening while Tiana was holding Louisa's hand and singing to her in her soft voice, she became overwhelmed with sadness. She got up from the bedside chair and left the house in tears. The next evening, she apologized for leaving without saying goodnight. Watching Louisa every night was heartbreaking for her as well as the family. She knew Louisa's time was short. Louisa died in her sleep shortly afterwards.

Louisa's burial was at St. Augustine's San Lorenzo Cemetery. It was on a bright sunny day. After the graveside services, the family was surrounded by friends at the St. Augustine Beach Embassy Suites. The banquet room was full of people who loved Louisa and Phillip. There was sadness in the air but also a sense of joy that Louisa was no longer suffering. Her soul has gone to a better place.

Two months later, Phillip got a text from Tiana asking how he was doing. A week later they had supper at Phillip's house. They talked about Louisa and the joyful moments they shared the past two years.

After more visits, conversation and suppers, Phillip became interested in Jamaican history. He told Tiana how similar it was to that of St. Augustine, especially the Spanish influence and the devastation of the indigenous populations.

The arrival of Spanish explorers in the New World was followed by the enslavement of indigenous people. This was customary practice for European nations expanding their territory and power in the world.

The customs and traditions of indigenous people were abolished. Their land was stolen. The Spanish explorers beginning with Christopher Columbus did not appreciate the tribes on the Caribbean islands. They viewed them as sub-humans. The indigenous populations were forced to convert to European religions. References to "enslaving people and fighting over god" may be found in most bibles. Conflicts based on "my god is better than your god" have always existed and still do.

Phillip told Tiana that Christopher Columbus thought he had reached India on his first voyage. That is why he named the indigenous people Indians. He sought gold and silver to finance a fifth Crusade to free the Holy Lands from the Muslims.

The Muslims committed atrocities on Christians when they seized Jerusalem in 636 A.D. In 1099 A.D., the Christian Crusaders won Jerusalem back. This time the Christians slaughtered Muslims and Jews including women and children. (This history is part of the reason for continuing hate between the Christians and Muslims as manifested through suicide bombers and other acts of terror on innocent men, women, and children.)

Eighty-eight years later, Muslim leader Saladin defeated the Crusaders. Muslims once again controlled Jerusalem. There was a fourth Crusade to free Jerusalem and the holy sites in 1291 A.D., but it failed. After the Muslims' victory, all Christians in the Holy Land were expelled.

The Ottoman Empire held the Holy Land for centuries. It backed Germany during World War I and when Germany was defeated, what was the Empire was redrawn by European victors.

Now the Church of the Holy Sepulcher and the Dome of the Rock are open to all and will be as long as Israel and Palestine keep peace in Jerusalem.

The Spanish colonists who settled Jamaica after the last Columbus voyage in 1502 enslaved the Taino tribes. These peaceful people, who had lived in Jamaica for thousands of years, were wiped out within five decades. There were only 200 Taino remaining on the island in 1542. Soon, all would be gone.

Not all died by the sword or harsh punishments. Jamaica was called an island of death because of tropical diseases, especially those borne by mosquitoes. The diseases Europeans brought with them such as smallpox, dysentery, measles and whooping-cough killed countless indigenous people.

Bartolome de Las Casas was a Dominican missionary and historian during this time period. He authored books on the history of the West Indies and described the harsh and evil treatment of Indians by Spanish explorers. Phillip and Tiana read a great deal of his stories in their search for her ancestors.

Members of the Carib tribe were described by some historians as cannibals. They crossed the waters from the island of Domenica on a regular basis to kill the Taino men and enslave the women. Historians believe the Caribs were cannibals because they placed human body parts on wooden devices for curing in the sun.

Other historians believe those body parts were intended to show the strength of the tribe, just as Native Americans in the American colonies displayed scalps from people they killed in battle. Columbus is thought by many to have defined the Caribs as cannibals so he could enslave them. Historians base this belief on his logbooks and stories written about him at the time.

The Caribs could have annihilated the Tainos over time, but the arrival of Spanish and British colonists expedited the process. Phillip told Tiana that indigenous tribes were wiped out in America the same as in Jamaica. Settlers wanted their land, and they took it. European powers in search of gold, silver, and spices in the name of their god killed millions of indigenous people all over the world because of their culture, religion, or the color of their skin.

"I saw the picture you sent me of the anchor from one of the ships Columbus sailed to Jamaica on. It was lying in a field of grass and weeds," Phillip said. "If that anchor was in America, there would be a monument for it."

"Did you learn Jamaica's early history when you were in school?" he asked Tiana.

"Columbus was taught in some of

the history classes, but I can't remember being taught that slavery began with Columbus," she said. "Columbus should have obeyed Spain's instructions to treat the indigenous people fairly. I think it would have been easier to convert them to Catholicism through kindness rather than the sword. What do you think about Columbus?"

"I have been a member of the Knights of Columbus for 50 years. I'm not sure I would have joined as quickly had I known about Christopher Columbus and the dark side of his life," Phillip said.

"What do the Knights of Columbus do?" Tiana asked.

"The Knights help people. When it was chartered, it was the only fraternal group helping Catholic immigrants. Catholics were treated as harshly as any group of immigrants that ever migrated to America," he said. "The Philadelphia riots in 1840 for instance resulted in hatred and bitterness between Protestants and Catholics that may never heal completely. But relations have improved to the point that two Catholics have been elected as President of the United States. The Knights of Columbus is the largest Catholic fraternal organization in America. It is founded on the principles of charity, unity, fraternity, and patriotism. That is what it has always worked for during my time as an active member."

Phillip told Tiana about the anti-Catholic riot in Philadelphia on May 3, 1844. Protestant nativists who enforced a policy of protecting the interests of native inhabitants against those of immigrants destroyed dozens of Irish Catholic homes. They burned down schools and churches and attacked Catholics on the streets. The state militia was called in resulting in the death of several nativists. The mob was enraged because Irish and German Catholic immigrants moved into their neighborhoods. Religious hatred is always fierce.

In 1875, President Ulysses S. Grant recommended a constitutional amendment denying funds for sectarian schools. 'Sectarian' was the code word for Catholic. The proposal, known as the Blaine amendment, passed in the U.S. House of Representatives, but failed by four votes in the Senate.

There are still 37 states in America that have retained the essence of the Blaine amendment in their constitutions. It is used to defend policies that ban appropriations of public funds to private schools. In Florida, the lines are getting fuzzy on which schools are funded, what books can be in the library and what subjects taught. The state is being accused of keeping students away from critical thinking. Significant efforts are in the works to replace the public school system with charter schools controlled by the private sector. There are extremists trying to rewrite history all over

America. In Florida, these movements are epidemic.

The most anti-Catholic governor elected in Florida was Sidney J. Catts (1917-1921). He was a shrewd Alabama-born man who capitalized on the anti-Catholic sentiment growing in Florida even though only 12% of the population was Catholic. The majority of them lived in St. Augustine. Catts ran on an anti-Catholic/anti-immigration platform. It's the same political plan that has been part of American culture since the founding of the first colony in 1607 by people determined to avoid all contact with Papists, as Catholics have been called since the Reformation.

The Ku Klux Klan was powerful during reconstruction after the Civil War and years afterwards. This malevolent group wanted Jews, Catholics and people of color removed from American society. They wanted a white protestant country that never was and never will be. The majority of Americans believe in freedom of religion and would never accept a state religion.

"That was a great history lesson," Tiana said.

In the West Indies, one nation attempted to remove all white people. The Haiti Massacre took place in 1804.

Jean-Jacques Dessalines, the self-proclaimed emperor of Haiti, decided to rid the country of all white blood. Dessalines spent years as a slave under brutal owners. He served as second in command to the governor when Haiti switched its allegiance from Spain to France. When France decided to reinstate slavery in Haiti, Dessalines led his troops in fierce fighting and drove the French out. The Dessalines-led massacre wiped out 5,000 French Creoles of all ages, men and women, as revenge for the blood-curdling atrocities French landowners committed on Haitian slaves.

The tortures utilized by the French slave owners were unspeakable.

In 1805, only non-whites could own land and be citizens of Haiti. Dessalines was the leader of the first nation to abolish slavery.

A Haitian document at the U.S. Library of Congress says when Haiti declared its independence, Dessalines' secretary Boisrond-Tonnerre said, "For our declaration of independence, we should have the skin of a white man for parchment, his skull for an inkwell, his blood for ink, and a bayonet for a pen!"

"That's about all the history you need for today," Phillip said.

Phillip amused Tiana when he tried his best to learn Patwah.

"When you are speaking Patwah, the words come from an unknown alphabet and are incoherent to the human ear," she said.

Phillip laughed and said, "Everting gwin be irie," a phrase he learned from Brad Pitt's character in the movie, "Meet Joe Black." Tiana tossed a soft pillow at him because she and Louisa had heard him use that line more than a hundred times.

Phillip and Tiana usually get take-out from restaurants. They met four times a week for supper and company. Tiana sometimes cooked Jamaican dishes. Her ox-tail recipe with peas, rice and fried plantains was delicious.

They made one-day trips to New Smyrna, Daytona Beach and Bunnell on the weekend. Spending time with Tiana in the car got Phillip through the rawest hours of his grieving. He told her he would always be grateful for her company during those hard times.

After a month, the car trips and meals at the house had become a regular event, and Phillip's daughter Clara asked him, "Daddy, are you dating

Tiana Bennett?"

Phillip answered with a firm "No" and a laugh. When he told Tiana his daughter asked if they were dating, she laughed as heartily as he did. They joked about dating for a week or so, and then Phillip called Tiana one afternoon and asked if he could take her to Dude's Seafood Café at Flagler Beach for dinner. She accepted.

" I guess we are having a date," he said. "Is five-o'clock a suitable time for you?"

"Our first date," she said with a laugh. "See you at five."

Phillip told his son Leo he hoped his relationship with Tiana wasn't causing any angst for the family. Surely, they realize that Tiana was able to come visit on a regular basis because everyone else was busy leading their own lives. She helped Phillip make it through some dark times. What anyone outside the family thought about his friendship with Tiana was of no concern to Phillip. And it was his feeling that if he spent time with a lady who brings him joy, the family should support that special and unique friendship.

Phillip talks to Louisa every morning, every evening, and during the day when he walks through the house looking at pictures of her. He reads the Liturgy of the Hours every morning and every night. He sits in his leather chair looking at the beautiful picture of Louisa on the shelf. They were in New Orleans for Pope John Paul's visit on Sept. 12, 1987 when it was taken.

Phillip tells Louisa his prayers are for her. He prays she is in the presence of the Lord and in the warmth of being Home. He tells her what he is doing, and feels she is sitting by him as she always did.

He tells her about his relationship with Tiana Bennett. He said he was wondering if she sent Tiana to see how he managed a unique friendship. He told her it sounds like something she would do to ease his pain. He feels Louisa is smiling.

Phillip and Tiana's relationship developed as a product of more than two years spent together taking care of an incredibly special loved one. After telling Louisa that he misses her and loves her, he looked up "friendship" in the Britannica dictionary.

"Friendship is a state of enduring affection, esteem, intimacy, and trust between two people."

Phillip rose from the chair, headed to the bedroom, and said to himself, "That sounds about right."

Chapter Three

AFTER HELPING GRAMMA WASH AND DRY THE DISHES, POTS, AND PANS IN THE HOT WATER THEY HEATED ON THE WOOD STOVE, TIANA AND ALEIYA GAVE HER A KISS. "I hope we have corn cakes tonight," Tiana said. "I have not had any in a long time."

Tiana sat in the front seat and Aleiya sat in the back for the ride to Oracabessa Bay in Grandpa's bright blue 10-year-old Toyota wagon. They managed the potholes in the road thanks to the sponge cushions he had placed on the seats a couple of years ago. His Toyota had made this same trip for the last five years. Grandpa tells anyone who will listen that it is the best car he has ever owned. He confidently drives up or down any hill in Jamaica even when the car is loaded with his fish traps and fishing gear.

They found a parking place next to the bay. Grandpa pulled Tiana aside and gave her a hug. He whispered in her ear, "Brantley called me yesterday. He told me he was in town and wants to get his papers back."

Tiana's body stiffened.

"That bastard," she said in a faint voice, her teeth clenched and anger rising. Tiana never wanted to see him again. He was one of the reasons she had moved to St. Augustine.

She stared at Grandpa's bearded, wrinkled face and regained her composure, then turned to Aleiya and said, "Cum Aleiya cum wi ave a fun day pan di bay."

"I thought we were going to speak English," Aleiya said with a laugh as they got into the crowded mini-bus to Blue Hole Park.

Brantley Baxter was Chandice Bennett's father. Tiana and Baxter lived together under common law in Jamaica. Chandice has never met him. If Tiana has her way, she never will meet the man. She refers to him only as "the bastard."

Baxter fled St. Mary Parish two weeks before Chandice was born without saying a word to Tiana. Tiana never talks about him in front of Chandice. If his name comes up, she changes the subject or leaves the room. He was a *ganja* dealer before Tiana became pregnant, something she did not know about when the sweet talking and the dating had begun. Tiana lived with Baxter less than a year.

After Baxter left St. Mary, he set up his drug business in Kingston where his suppliers were. Baxter pocketed $150 in U.S. dollars every day he made deliveries.

Baxter was known on the streets as a "dependable mon" who delivered the good stuff. He was approached about joining a cocaine, crack and heroin organization doing business in New York City. They saw Baxter was satisfied with his small territory operation and concluded that he was not ready for the big time.

Bad people in high places knew who Baxter was and kept an eye on him. There was no way he could expand his drug-peddling business on his own unless he left Jamaica. He knew he would be rubbed out if he crossed the ringleaders.

Tiana's phone vibrated and Baxter's name appeared. Blood rushed to her head, her eyes narrowed and her skin crawled. She declined the call. Aleiya asked her if everything was all right. She nodded yes and said, "No problem."

Tiana knew that what Baxter wanted most of all was to get her in bed. That was always the first thing on his mind. That would never happen again. Besides his desire for sex, he wanted to recover an envelope that he had hidden in the lining of Tiana's suitcase.

The records in the envelope could put him and his clients in jeopardy.

Baxter knew that Grandpa Bennett would beat the crap out of him if he came around his house. And, Tiana had obtained a restraining order against him. He could be jailed if he were caught near her. At five-foot-six inches tall and a slight 140 pounds, he was not about to go to Tiana's house and take on Grandpa Bennett. In any event, he wasn't the kind of man to get his hands, clothes or shoes dirty. He was *gyalis* in the truest sense of the word.

Baxter was not a mean person. He smoked ganja from time to time and would drink a beer or two, but he always wanted to remain in control and know where he was and where the closest exit was located. He did not own a gun, but always carried his chopper on his belt. His father had given him the special knife when he was 10 years old, and he knew how to use it.

Chapter Four

TIANA SPENT FOUR HOURS LOOKING THROUGH
BOXES OF FILES AT THE JAMAICA HISTORICAL
FOUNDATION. She saw an article that ex-
plained that the name Jamaica comes
from Haymaca, an indigenous name
that means "Island of Fountains."

The staff at the Foundation was
most helpful. The entire department
became interested in her work when
she told them why she had moved to
America's oldest permanently settled
city. She told them there were indi-
cations her seven-great grandfather
had migrated from St. Augustine to
Jamaica as a British loyalist and now
she had reversed his steps.

Tiana discovered few clues in the
Jamaican historical records, but she
discovered in an internet search that

there exist passenger records of people arriving in Jamaica after the American War of Independence. The names of people who had been on the British ships might be in Salt Lake City, Utah.

A sad fact she and the staff discovered was that while most loyalists suffered considerable social and financial hardship, conditions were even worse for Black loyalists, thousands of whom died in Canada and England of poverty and poor health. Tiana was upset to learn some Black loyalists who had earned their freedom were sold again as slaves in the Caribbean. The fierce fighting they endured for Mother England had been for naught. She had turned her backs on them.

Tiana prayed that her ancestor had not been made a slave. If he had made it to Jamaica as a free man because he fought to bring the Bahamas back under the King's colors, his name should be listed somewhere.

After she finished her research, Tiana stayed with her grandparents and visited friends in the close-knit community for the rest of the week. She poured her love into Gramma, Grandpa and Aleiya. At the end of her stay, she caught a mid-morning flight to Miami. She wanted to be back in St. Augustine and to see Phillip.

She called Phillip from the Kingston airport and told him when she would be home, assuming she made her connection in Miami. There was a good chance that she would because she had a two- hour layover.

"Hello Phillip," she said. "I should be home around 4 o'clock."

"That's great Tiana. May I pick you up for fresh fried shrimp at O'Steen's?" Phillip said.

"What a treat that would be if we can get a table," she enthused.

"If it's too crowded, we can try

Schooner's or that new place by the King Street bridge. We can sit on the deck and watch the sun go down on the San Sebastian River," he said.

"It's a date, even if it's a platonic one," she said with a tiny giggle. "I'm glad your family accepts our friendship."

"LOL," he said. "You are a mess. All they want is for their daddy to be as happy as possible. They know you make me smile, and you know it too. See you at 7."

The line at O'Steen's world famous shrimp restaurant on Anastasia Island extended to the back end of the building. Older folks waited in parked cars to avoid the strain of standing.

Tiana and Phillip decided to go to the St. Augustine Seafood Company restaurant on King Street. The wait there was a manageable 45 minutes. They walked down to the edge of the river near where S. Salvador and Sons had had their fish house years ago. Across the river, little remained of the Fazio shrimp docks; there, a massive hotel was under construction.

Phillip told Tiana what shrimping had been like in St. Augustine before and after World War II. He said he would take her to the shrimp industry monument when they had more time. Phillip knew very well the Italian families that dominated the St. Augustine fishing industry all those years.

When he was in the masonry trade, Philip had poured hundreds of yards of concrete for the Ringhaver family at their shrimp boat building facility further down the San Sebastian River. More offshore shrimp trawlers were built in St. Augustine than any other place in the United States. Diesel Engine Sales created hundreds of good paying jobs and contributed to the economic survival of St. Augustine during rough years. Tiana liked learning about the seafood industry's historical impacts on her new hometown.

Phillip's name was called by the hostess, and they followed her to a table that was away from the water in the darker part of the restaurant. The restaurant was full of tourists, along with a few local people that Phillip spoke or nodded to.

Roger Smith, one of Phillip's masonry friends, stopped at Phillip's table on his way back from the men's room. He put his hand on Phillip's shoulder and told him how sorry he was for his loss of Louisa. Phillip stood, shook his hand, and thanked him for his kind words. He introduced Tiana Bennett to Roger, calling her a friend.

There was no need to provide Roger with more information about his beautiful Jamaican companinon, and he did not do so. Roger, ever the gentleman, smiled at Tiana and shook her hand. "Nice to meet you," he said, then headed back to his table. For many years, he had been used to seeing Phillip with Louisa.

As Roger sat down, his wife asked, "Who is that woman with Phillip?"

"Her name is Tiana Bennett," he answered.

"Who is Tiana Bennett?" she asked Roger, then looked at the couple who were sitting with them at the table.

"Beats me," they replied.

Roger's guests glanced at Phillip and Tiana for the rest of their meal. Phillip smiled at them each time he caught them looking. Tiana asked him why he was smiling, and he merely smiled at her, too.

After dining on scrumptious cheese grits, wild-caught fried shrimp, and Hull's crab cakes, Phillip and Tiana decided to ride to St. Augustine Beach and visit the posh Embassy Suites Hotel. They planned to splurge on one of their world-class desserts. The valet made sure the key fob for Phillip's Ford Raptor was on the console when he opened the door for Tiana.

They strolled side by side through the grand lobby and headed downstairs to the outside beach chairs. They loved to watch and listen to the waves breaking on the beach. When the server arrived, they ordered a piece of Death by Chocolate cake and two cups of black coffee.

There was music in the air. A cool evening breeze came whispering off the South Atlantic ocean and the sky was alive with stars. Phillips and Tiana were surrounded by people in a happy place.

Tiana touched Phillip's hand and asked, "Did you ever watch 'How Stella Got Her Groove Back' while I was in Jamaica?"

"I sure did," he said looking into her brown eyes. "You were right about a couple of those scenes that were rated 'X' in 1998."

Tiana laughed and said, "In 2022 those scenes are probably rated G."

They both chuckled.

"You remember when I told you I had an R-rated dream about you," Phillip asked.

"I do," she said.

"One of the scenes in the movie depicted my dream."

"What scene was that if you don't mind me asking?"

Phillip took a long moment to respond. He was not prepared to share all of the details of his dream.

"The scene most like my dream was Stella washing Winston's back in the steaming shower," he said as he blushed. "Except I am doing the washing."

Tiana looked at him without saying anything. She smiled and squeezed his hand.

Tiana arrived at her office an hour early. She had a bounce in her step.

She knew that after spending a week in Jamaica, she would be confronting a full inbox. Co-workers began arriving and wanted to know what kind of fun she had had during her trip. She said she would fill them in on the visit at lunch but did say she had an enjoyable time with family and discovered valuable information about her ancestor who sailed from St. Augustine to Jamaica.

Everybody in the office were friends with one another and shared what they did when not at work. All were delighted to learn about the progress Tiana was making with her family history project.

Phillip was also energized that morning. He was always happy when he had inside work at Flagler College. The work had to be performed slowly and perfectly. The college maintenance crew built him a sturdy scaffold that rolled from place to place in the expansive ballroom. They installed a step ladder to make it easier for Phillip to climb to the top of the scaffold. He appreciated them for making his work easier and safer. They knew he was 75. None of this would have been necessary when he was 65. He had all day to re-plaster portions of cracked plaster surrounding the chandeliers.

Phillip and Tiana were going to study the papers she brought back from Jamaica that night. He was going to compile all of the data he could gather from his Ancestry.com accounts concerning Jamaicans in the War for Independence.

Phillip arrived at Tiana's house at 6:30 with shrimp perlow made by his friends Sonny and Barry. His sister Lessie had prepared a chef salad for them. He got two big hugs from Tiana when she saw the Minorcan food.

Phillip had made Lessie aware of

Tiana's history project, and she knew all about the project and their friendship.

Almost 10,000 Southern loyalists fled to Jamaica from Florida and more from other states. One article indicated that fewer than 200 white loyalists left St. Augustine for Jamaica. White slave owners from Georgia and the Carolinas brought their slaves with them. African Americans who were free and had been loyal to the British Crown during the War had free passage to Canada, Jamaica, or England.

Jamaica was Britain's most profitable colony in the West Indies. It had fertile land and an abundance of slaves to work it. After the American War of Independence ended, life for a white loyalist in Jamaica was far easier than it was for a Black loyalist. British culture was not ready for an influx of free Blacks.

Tiana learned the migration of Black loyalists from America to Jamaica brought about the spread of the Baptist faith throughout the island. The first ordained Black Baptist minister was George Liele. He was a big part of the Baptist evangelization movement. Liele was born a slave in Virginia but freed by his owner before the War for Independence began. Liele was jailed in Jamaica for sedition. To the Jamaican authorities, his sermons sounded more like insurrection than religion.

Phillip told Tiana if her ancestors had been loyalists there was a chance that they were members of the Baptist church that had grown due to Liele's work. Parishes within the church recorded births, marriages, and deaths on registers. Tiana and Phillip needed to search those records for soldier/loyalists.

By 11 p.m., they had not found anything new. Both had to be at work early the morning. Standing at the front door Philip said, "We have a unique relationship, don't we?"

"We certainly have become good friends. It is natural. We were in the same house giving loving care to your wife for over two years," Tiana said. "Why do you ask?"

"My son Leo got a call from one of his friends the other day expressing sympathy for Louisa's passing, and the friend then asked how I was doing. Leo said he chuckled and then reported, 'Oh, he's doing OK. We believe he's dating a 40-year-old Jamaican lady, and they are having fun. As a matter of fact, I think they were at Flagler Beach last night eating seafood at Dude's seafood restaurant.'"

"In addition, my daughter Clara was visiting one of her college friends in Arizona last week and we came up in their conversation," Phillip told Tiana. "They were talking about kids, art, and life in general. Clara's friend told her how sorry she was that her mother died. She asked if her dad was at a retirement village playing shuffleboard and checkers with other senior citizens. Clara broke into a very loud laugh."

Actually, Clara said, "He will be 76 in four months. He is considering doing more brick work for the historical organizations and building an outdoor kitchen at his house. He has developed a relationship with Tiana Bennett, a 40-year-old Jamaican woman who was one of mom's caregivers. Right now, they are making day trips to places near St. Augustine. No overnight trips or anything like that," she said.

"Tell me more" her friend said.

"I don't believe there's romance as we define it, but they do enjoy each other's company," she said. "Dad said she makes him feel good. From what I have seen she enjoys his company. It's not like Dad went to a bar to find somebody to be with. He and Tiana have been visiting, talking, laughing, kidding, and learning about each other's culture for years. He certainly doesn't let the age difference hinder anything at all."

"Oh, Clara that friendship must be so good for soothing his grief," her friend said.

"My dad is unique," Clara continued. "He says his insurance consultant refers to him as an actuarial anomaly. He's almost 76, weighs 250 pounds and according to the insurance actuarial chart, he died fifteen years ago."

They both laughed.

"What a wonderful story. I'm so glad you told me," her friend said. "Your dad is living his life to the fullest and doing things his way. I am glad he is living in the moment."

"I totally agree," Clara said.

Tiana rolled her eyes and gave Phillip a peck on the cheek. He hugged her and said goodnight. She locked the door after she heard the Raptor roar to life and pull out of the driveway.

Chapter Five

TIANA AND PHILLIP WERE SEARCHING FILES AND DOCUMENTS WHEN THEY READ THAT MORE THAN 25,000 BRITISH LOYALISTS AND THEIR SLAVES MIGRATED TO JAMAICA. They were not welcomed by Jamaican plantation owners who had been prospering for years on the backs of slaves who worked and lived under harsh conditions. The original sugar plantation owners did not want competition and they were beginning to worry about becoming outnumbered by black people. However, the British Parliament was fully committed to slavery and said they would help manage the new arrivals.

Tiana read what historian Patrick E. Brady wrote to Phillip.

Both refugees and migrants comprised the Loyalist exile to Jamaica. Whether one was a refugee or migrant was determined by their social and economic status during the war. Those with substantial means and connections could afford to emigrate from the colonies to avoid substantial losses. Those with less means remained in British-occupied cities until the war ended in 1783, then relied on paternalistic officials to cover their evacuation. The former were slaveowners who chose to migrate to Jamaica, where they could rebuild their lives using enslaved labor. The Jamaican Assembly later contested the aid claims of these "free migrants," citing their lack of legitimate need for protection. The Assembly treated poor Loyalists as deserving of alms since their emigration from the American colonies was involuntary. Most poor refugees, if given a choice, would have chosen anywhere other than Jamaica. The island's reputation as a black hole of disease and slave rebellion was legendary. Further, the poor did not possess the capital, knowledge, or resources to become planters. They wanted to keep their family and limbs intact through their ordeal. Thus, the paradox of choice and deservingness shaped the postwar experiences of Loyalists. A barrage of hurricanes, slave revolts, imperial wars, and disease including the 1793 yellow fever epidemic pulled the slave society to its knees. Loyalists observed the society buckle as the contradictions of paternalism and slavery became unmanageable.

These were extremely tough times throughout the West Indies. Fiery rhetoric about freedom and equality and the success of American patriots lifting the yoke of British rule from their shoulders inspired other nations in the Caribbean to seek their own independence. Britain was so deep in the slave trade that it did not prohibit the practice until 1834. The brutal treatment of slaves at some Jamaican plantations lasted until 50 years after the American revolution.

Tiana was learning Jamaican history she was never taught in school. She wondered why students were not taught historical truth.

She found a document proving there was a migration of British loyalists from St. Augustine to Jamaica. She yearned to know if her ancestor migrated to Jamaica from St. Augustine as a British soldier or as a slave of a British loyalist.

Phillip has attended Alcohol Anonymous meetings for 25 years. He was recently recognized for his commitment to the program. He attends the 7 p.m. meetings at Our Lady of Good Council Catholic Church on the F. Charles Usina Highway that runs from I-95 east to San Marco Avenue. The highway was named by the Florida Legislature to honor Phillip's Minorcan relative.

Phillip never considered himself an alcoholic even though he drank every night. He felt he could manage himself and detested anyone suggesting he had a drinking problem. It was standard procedure when he was young and in the masonry trade that on Friday he and his friends gathered at the Tradewinds Bar. The cry of a bricklayer was, "Thank God for payday and 5 o'clock." This ritual continued after he married Louisa Oliveros on a beautiful May day in 1972.

Louisa said it was good for him to have a change of pace because he worked like a Trojan. He deserved time with friends they had both known since elementary school. After their second child was born, they were getting ready to go to Mass one Sunday at the Cathedral when Louisa said, " I wish you would come home earlier on Fridays to help me."

"I don't think I spend too much time away from home," he answered.

"I know honey," she said. "But times have changed. We have a family to raise. I need your help."

Phillip resented Louisa's request. He did not raise his voice, but Louisa saw the expression on his face and the hurt in his eyes.

Alcoholics Anonymous defines alcoholism as "a physical compulsion, coupled with a mental obsession to consume alcohol, in which cravings for alcohol are always catered to, even at times when they should not be."

Phillip never drank in secrecy, but he craved a drink every day after work — just a beer or two which turned into three or four.

After more conversation with Louisa about Friday night happy hours, he began feeling guilty. He was spending hard earned money for scotch and water instead of being home and providing necessities for Louisa and the kids. The way Phillip figured things, he worked hard and was entitled to some times with the boys. Only later in life, when he stopped drinking, did he realize that Louisa was working as hard as he was raising the children and running the house. He was thinking only about himself.

Over the years Phillip's drinking became more obvious at home. His friends had moved to other cities. Friday nights weren't the same. He lived up to his responsibilities as a father. He loved Louisa more than anything in the world and everyone knew it.

He joined the Matanzas River Fishing Club and the Moose Club and began going to VFW meetings. Having drinks afterwards became routine. He often staggered to bed but always with a smile on his face. Phillip was a happy drunk who considered himself a lover not a fighter. In truth, after 20 years of his drinking addiction, he was neither.

One evening he had too many cocktails but refused to let friends take him home. He left the bar's parking lot and decided to go wading at St. Augustine Beach. He made the turn at the west end of the Bridge of Lions, then passed out. His Chevy truck crashed into the marble lion on the south side of the bridge. The next thing he remembered was waking up in a bed at Flagler Hospital surrounded by friends and a policeman who had known him all his life.

Phillip blinked his eyes. He looked at Louisa who was gently sobbing. "Where am I?" he said. "How did I get here?"

"Oh, Phillip," she said. "Thank God you are okay. I love you so much."

The following day Sgt. Bill Cassidy visited Phillip and gave him a citation to appear in court for driving under the influence and damaging city property. After Cassidy handed him the citation, he took his hat off and sat down beside the bed. He and Phillip talked about all their good times in high school for over an hour. They laughed and they cried when they talked about the friends who were no longer alive.

Phillip hired one of St. Augustine's best defense attorneys. Hamilton Upton told him his offense was a misdemeanor because it was his first offense. Punishment could include imprisonment in the county jail for up to six months, or the court could choose to sentence a defendant to probation for one year and 50 hours of community work. Fines ranged between $500 and $2,000 plus court costs depending on the facts of the case and the mood of the judge. DUI first offenders were required to attend a state-approved DUI school program.

Phillip stared at the ceiling. He told Hamilton what an irresponsible fool he had been.

"I can certainly do all of that if required. Fifty hours picking up trash around town will be humbling. I know how embarrassed Louisa and the family will be. I feel like I have never felt before."

"Yes, you were a dumb-ass," Hamilton replied. "But I say a lucky dumb-ass. You could have killed innocent people. You could have killed yourself and what would happen to Louisa? Blessed are you for passing out at minimum speed when few other cars were on the road, and nobody was walking on the sidewalk near the bridge."

"I'm afraid to ask Ham, but is there any way I can still drive to work?"

Hamilton smiled. He knew that question was coming.

"I have filed an SR-22 form and I

believe the court will grant you a hard-ship license during your three-year driver's license suspension."

Hamilton saw a tear roll down Phillip's cheek, shook his hand, then left the room. That moment and that conversation served as Phillip's 'Road to Damascus' conversion. He never touched a drop of alcohol from that day on.

Chapter Six

TIANA AND PHILLIP DISCUSSED HOW LIFE IN JAMAICA COMPARED TO LIFE IN ST. AUGUSTINE. Phillip asked Tiana if there were many white people in her life before she moved to St. Augustine. She told him she never saw a white person for the first 10 years of her life. There were no white people in her community. The first time she saw a white person was in Oracabessa by Sea. She was in town shopping with her grandmother when she saw four white tourists. Nobody taught her to dislike white people or any people because of the color of their skin. White people simply weren't part of her life. It was different in Kingston, Montego Bay, and other tourist-oriented cities, but not in the country communities.

Tiana said migrating to America was a bittersweet experience. The emigre leaves behind everything she is familiar with and the people she loves. She has no idea what she will be facing next. Tiana had other reasons, but she moved mostly because the opportunity to achieve economic freedom was far better in the United States.

Phillip asked her, "What was the picture of America in your mind before you came here the first time?"

"My picture of America was no potholes, no bushes, no homeless," she said.

"What you got was potholes, bushes and homeless," Phillip said with a laugh.

"Yes, but the potholes are not as deep or as many," she said.

Phillip asked Tiana if she experienced racism when she and Chandice arrived in St. Augustine. She told him there were no incidents in her day-to-day life during the first year. She lived with her mother on Saragossa Street in a rented two-story house built in the 1800s. She also worked for her uncle at his Jamaican restaurant on San Marco Avenue. Her world was small, but easy. She loved hearing her mom call her Yanigue again.

Philip wanted to learn more about what people of color live with every day in a society dominated by whites. He disliked people for whom "making America great again" equated to "making America white again."

Tiana said she has learned to live with racism and to accept that there is no way to change the hearts and minds of people who believe people of color are inferior.

Phillip never hated anyone because of the color of the skin, where they worked or what their outlook on religion was. He tried to treat others like he wanted to be treated. He was not successful all the time, but the effort to do the right thing for the right reason was always there.

After Tiana shared her racial experiences, she asked Philip what race relations were like when he was growing up in St. Augustine and when he first perceived that there was a divide between white people and people of color.

Phillip put his glass of water on the table and paused for a moment.

"That's hard to answer Tiana," he said. "When I was growing up on Vilano Beach and North City, I did not think about race relations. I did not think about all my friends being white. I went to a church with only white people and to public schools with white people. I did not have any Black friends. There was no feeling of hate or dislike on my part. I definitely had no knowledge of what Black people were going through."

St. Augustine was home to slaves when it was founded, but the number of slaves in St. Augustine under the Spanish flag was significantly smaller than the populations of slaves in British colonies, especially Georgia, the Carolinas and Virginia. Large plantations needed a steady source of cheap slave labor to survive. Britain businessmen supplied them.

St. Augustine was not a British colony until 1763. British occupation lasted until 1783 when the colonists prevailed in the American War of Independence. During those 20 years of British rule, slave ownership within their empire grew so high Britain became the largest and most profitable slave trading nation in the world.

From 1565 to 1763 St. Augustine was under the Spanish flag. According to the *East Florida Gazette* and government documents, Spain was more interested in converting indigenous people to

Catholicism than making them slaves for sale.

Spain built a series of Catholic missions in Florida, Georgia, and South Carolina. The missions were established in locations where language barriers were relatively easy to overcome.

One of the most outspoken opponents of the missions was Gov. James Moore of South Carolina. He sent men capable of great cruelty to destroy all the Spanish Missions in the Florida Panhandle and South Georgia. His mercenaries slaughtered innocent men, women and children and enslaved over a thousand of the survivors. Moore's men marched the captives to South Carolina to work plantations until they died or escaped. Phillip said these men were the worst of the worst.

"When I became a bricklayer in St. Augustine, I knew of no Black masons," Phillip said. "There may have been Black bricklayers and plasterers working in the Black community, but I did not think about that. I was too concerned about working every day because in the trade if you don't work you don't get paid. If you don't get paid you don't eat".

"We had Black laborers who mixed the mortar, toted the blocks, dug footings, poured concrete and other necessary tasks. We could not have built anything without them, but there was never a Black brick layer or plas-terer on the scaffold with me."

"Had you ever thought about this before?" she asked.

"Not really," he said. "My friends believed in live and let live. Nobody I knew wanted to harm somebody be-cause of the color of their skin. But in those days, if you were Black, you had to sit in the balcony of the Matanzas theater. Downstairs was for white people. Black people had their separate entrance on Charlotte Street. I did not pay any attention to this. It was the way it always had been. I did not make things that way, the Southern white society made them that way, now that I'm thinking about it," he said.

Phillip was 17 years old when President Lyndon Johnson signed one of the most important and controversial laws ever enacted. It had a profound impact on St. Augustine and communities throughout the nation.

He was in high school when the peaceful demonstrations led by the Rev. Martin Luther King began in St. Augustine.

"None of us in our neighborhood went downtown because of the trouble going on," Phillip said. "Certain elements of people in St. Augustine were angry that Black people demanded equality and the ability to go anywhere white people went and to work at any job that was open. Segregation was in full bloom in the nation's oldest city. The issue must be continuously addressed by the citizens of St. Augustine if equal justice under law is to prevail," he said.

The Ku Klux Klan arrived in St. Augustine spewing hatred and violence but was kept in check by law enforcement officers. The Civil Rights Act of 1964, signed into law by a man from Texas, would change the world for the better. But it would be years before benefits of the Civil Rights Act were codified as law felt by Black communities.

"I am old enough and hopefully wise enough to understand we should never hate anyone because of the color of their skin," Phillips said. "Hatred of someone or a group or religion you don't know much about has to be taught. In today's world, all a person has to do is listen to programming that spews hatred, division, blame and guilt seven days a week."

"There is no way to change a person's paradigm if he only listens to one set of commentators," Tiana said.

"People should understand the bottom line in all of this is for the corporations to make money. Individual and corporate egos have to have an enemy," Phillip said. "There has to be somebody or some group to hate. That allows the ego to function as it wishes. Ego is the False Self in all of us. Hagar the Horrible, once said in a comic strip, 'Friends come and friends go, but a good enemy will last a lifetime.' Hatred of 'them' works well in politics."

"I never heard that statement before, but it is true and that motto happens every day on cable news," she said. "Why do you think so many people hate Muslims?"

"That's interesting that you ask," he said. I was working on a job two years ago building a motel on St. Augustine Beach. At noon we all sat down in the shade behind a finished wall for our 30-minute lunch break. One of the men in the group, he may have been a plumber or tile setter, started the conversation by saying he was concerned about Sharia law coming to St. Augustine."

"What are you talking about?" I asked.

"They are going to put Sharia law in effect and we are going to have to live under a new set of Muslin laws."

"Where did you hear that?" I said.

"It's all over the news," he said.

"How in the world could people who want to live under Sharia law get it passed by our city and county commissioners?" I asked.

"They can just do it," he said.

"No, they, whoever they are, cannot change our laws just because a bobble-head on TV said they can. The only way Sharia law can become law in St. Johns County is to elect county commissioners who support Sharia law. There is no way a person advocating Sharia law could be elected in St. Johns County or in any other county in Florida."

"Well, you know how those Muslins are," he said testily.

"Actually, I don't know because I have never met more than two Muslims in my life."

"Well, I saw three of them in a grocery store last week and they looked different. They had rags around their head and they were speaking a funny language," he said.

"Were they pushing a grocery cart and buying goods the same as you?"

"I suppose so," he said.

"How many Muslims do you think are in St. Augustine?"

" Well, I don't know but I have seen a couple," he said.

"Do you think a couple of Muslims are going to change our state and federal laws and insert Sharia law?"

"I don't know, but it concerns me," he said.

Moving to get back on the scaffold, I said, "If I am in a grocery store and I see Muslims buying groceries with their family, I'm going over to them and say hello and welcome to America. Glad you are here."

Racism divides America. Creating distrust and fear of people who are "not like us" is a tactic dictators and autocrats have always used. Phillip and Tiana agreed racism was something they could not stop. What they could do was lead their lives without degrading anyone. They believed that if people came together for civil and frank discussions on racism there would be progress over time. They believed there were more good people than hatemongers in St. Augustine. Phillip's Minorcan friends simply wanted to live their lives as peacefully and happily as possible.

There are hundreds of millions of people in America who want to get along with everyone. Others, full of hate, chaos and confrontation. They have no shame about what they say or do.

Tiana and Phillip found a way to combat stress and anxiety by going to places that are quiet and safe. Once there, they think about where they are at that moment in their lives. Their current favorite safe places are south St. Augustine Beach or the jetties on Vilano Beach. Watching waves come ashore with a breeze blowing in their faces is mesmerizing and rejuvenating. If a person can't enjoy contemplation watching the endless waves, then the gift of contemplation for that person is unavailable. Such moments make work and life enjoyable as it can be.

Chapter Seven

TIANA WAS SITTING AT THE KITCHEN TABLE READ-
ING EVERYTHING SHE HAD FOUND ABOUT BLACK
LOYALISTS MIGRATING TO ST. AUGUSTINE FROM
OTHER COLONIES HOPING TO FIND A SAFE HAVEN
AND SECURE PASSAGE TO JAMAICA OR ANOTHER
BRITISH COLONY. There were accounts of
the difficulty sailing ships had getting
into St. Augustine through the unsta-
ble treacherous inlet that changed in
response to heavy winds and strong
tides. Historical documents told sad
tales about lives lost when ships full of
fleeing loyalists ran aground and sank.
Refugees arrived at the St. Augustine
Inlet from other colonies only to drown
when their ships broke apart trying to
cross the bar.

There were less than one thousand
Minorcans in St. Augustine in 1783

and 1784 as the loyalists arrived day after day. The local population had great difficulty adjusting to thousands of people moving into their small city even on a temporary basis. There was not enough food, shelter, and clothing to go around. Loyalists, both Black and white, constructed huts from palmettos and pieces of wood. What a chaotic moment for the citizens of St. Augustine during this time of British upheaval.

However, the taverns and houses of ill-repute were full of sailors and locals singing, cussing, fighting, and dancing 24 hours a day. Men of the sea are going to find what they are looking for when they come to port — or fight trying. Force majeure.

Tiana perused records about Gen. Alexander Leslie transporting thousands of Black loyalists to Jamaica, St. Augustine, New York, and Halifax in 1782 from the Port of Charleston.

Leslie was a British brigadier general of great renown. He fought in numerous battles during the American War of Independence including the siege of Charleston. Tiana wondered if her ancestor was one of the Black loyalists taken to Jamaica by Leslie. It was a possibility.

Tiana read that in 1783, after it was known the American colonists would win the war, about 400 white families with their 5,000 slaves arrived in Jamaica. They said they would rather be under the king than under a new political system.

George Liele arrived in Jamaica during this time. He was born a slave in Virginia. He became a Christian in 1773. He was baptized by Matthew Moore, his white pastor, and was given his freedom by his owner Henry Sharp, a Baptist deacon. When Sharp died in the war, his heirs tried to make Liele a slave again. He was jailed until

he produced the required documenta-
tion with help from a Colonel Kirkland.

He and his family moved to Jamaica
in 1782 to spread the Gospel of Jesus.
He arrived in Jamaica as the indentured servant of Kirkland because he
had no funds for his transportation. He
worked at various jobs for two years,
paid his debt, then received a certifi-
cate of freedom for himself and his
family. He became a preacher of great
renown and baptized over 500 hundred people.

The government, after listening
to his fiery speeches, said he was a
seditionist and put him in jail. But no
accusers showed up for the trial and
he was freed. During his life in Jamaica
the number of Baptists rose from 8,000
to 20,000.

Author David Shannon sums up Liele's
ministry this way: "The Christianity
practiced by Liele was not limited to one
nation, colony, or ethnic group, but was

a faith found and spread through interaction with colonists and national leaders in the Americas and England. In turn, this broad vision of Christianity shaped and spread a variety of Christian experience that became widespread and influential in Black, white, and integrated congregations in Georgia, South Carolina, Jamaica, Nova Scotia, Sierra Leone, and beyond."

Tiana found Article 19 of the Covenant of the Anabaptist church that reads, "We hold, if a brother or sister should transgress any of these articles written in this Covenant so as to become a: swearer, a fornicator, or adulterer; a covetous person, an idolater, a railer, a drunkard, an extortioner or whore-monger; or should commit any abominable sin, and does not give satisfaction to the Church, according to the Word of God, he or she, shall be put away from among us, not to keep company, nor to eat with us."

Tiana read that Britain used Jamaica as a base for slaves withdrawn from the American colonies, primarily Georgia and the two Carolinas. Bringing these slaves to Jamaica added to the British labor force throughout the Caribbean. At the same time, it prevented the Colonists from coming by the labor they needed to grow and harvest food crops.

One instance of Britain's close ties with Jamaica was personified by Lord Charles Montagu, the lieutenant colonel commandant of the Duke of Cumberland's Regiment, who assembled a provincial battalion in South Carolina for service in Jamaica in 1781. The battalions were composed of Mulattoes and Black people. Tiana's ancestor could have served in one of those battalions. If that were the case, there would be records of his military service somewhere.

After the War of Independence ended, Jamaica received more British loyalists than any other island in the Caribbean. The loyalists from St. Augustine and east Florida arrived in 1784 and 1785. In one brief period, Britain sent about 10,000 people to Jamaica. Eighty percent were loyalists and 20 percent were slaves. Less than 200 loyalists sailed to Jamaica from St. Augustine.

It was at a period of significant hurricanes and droughts in Jamaica. Hurricanes hurt slaves the most because of their inadequate living quarters. One estimate Tiana discovered calculated that between 1780 and 1786, some 15,000 slaves died of starvation. Hurricanes and drought destroyed their fruit and vegetables. Britain allowed no trade with American colonies because of the war. America had once been Jamaica's major trading partner and supplier of food.

Britain ruled Jamaica as a colony from 1707-1962. Although Britain was bringing loyalists out of harm's way in America, it still advocated slavery. They did not abolish slavery until Aug. 1, 1834, even though a motion to do so was made by David Hartley in the British House of Commons in 1777.

Hartley said, "The slave trade was contrary to the laws of God and to the rights of man." He did not get a second to his motion, but a predicate was laid.

Twenty-nine years later on Jan. 1, 1863, President Abraham Lincoln issued the Emancipation Proclamation. The world would never be the same. Freedom for slaves and for people of color cannot be achieved unless they have economic freedom.

Trina read about the uprising of the Trelawny Maroons in 1783. They bitterly complained they were not being treated as human beings. Violence erupted after two Maroons were punished at a workhouse in Montego Bay. A longstanding arrangement with the government dictated that the two men should have been handed over to the Maroons for any discipline. The Maroons also wanted more land because their population was increasing. This did not sit well with the governor. He ignored them and a short war followed.

During the uprising, the Maroons had no chance to win. Britain sent 5,000 hardened troops to quell the revolt. Bloodhounds brought in from Cuba hunted down Maroons in hiding. Anyone capturing a Maroon received a bounty of 10 English pounds. Within months the Maroons surrendered. They were promised they could stay in Jamaica, but that promise was broken like so many others extended by European governments.

Hundreds of Maroons were transported to Sierra Leone by way of Nova Scotia. "Nanny of the Maroons" is Jamaica's only heroine. Her picture is on the $500 bill, which is called a nanny.

Tiana picked up her last file and read about the Baptist War of 1831-1832.

The conflict was also known as "Sam Sharp Rebellion, the Christmas Rebellion, the Christmas Uprising and the Great Jamaican Slave Revolt of 1831–32."

It was a rebellion that lasted for only 11 days, but it was vicious. It began the day after Christmas 1831 and involved about 25 percent of the slaves in Jamaica. A Baptist deacon was one of the leaders. After it was quelled, more than 300 slaves including both men and women were executed.

Samuel Sharp was a literate slave and had access to newspapers that published stories about efforts in England and elsewhere where abolitionists were successful in freeing slaves. He was a popular speaker, utterly enthusiastic about gaining freedom for all people everywhere. He is one of Jamaica's heroes. His picture is on the $50 note. He was hung by the British for what he believed in. The Baptist War pushed Britain further down the road toward emancipation for Jamaica and all of its colonies.

Sharpe was hung at a place known as Sam Sharpe Square in Montego Bay. The courage of the brave men and women who rose up in 1831 is still re-membered and celebrated in Jamaica today.

A dire notice from the commanding British general to the rebels concerning their insurrection was posted through-out the island.

Headquarters, Montego Bay,
January 2, 1832

Negroes!
You have taken up arms against your masters, and have burned and plundered their dwell-ings. Some wicked persons have told you that the King has made you free, and that your masters

withhold your freedom from you. In the name of the King, I come among you, to tell you that you have been misled. I bring with me numerous forces to punish the guilty, and all, who are found with the rebels, shall be put to death without mercy. You cannot resist the King's troops. Surrender yourselves and beg that your crimes may be pardoned. All who yield themselves up at any military post immediately, provided they are not principles and chiefs in the burnings that have been committed, will receive His Majesty's greatest pardon; all who hold out will meet with certain death.

Willoughby G. Cotton
Major-General Commanding

Tiana put her files back neatly in a box, shook her head and called Phillip.

Chapter Eight

"IS IT TOO LATE TO GET A CUP OF COFFEE AT YOUR HOUSE?" Tiana said.

"It is never too late to have coffee with you," Phillip said. "I'll come get you, so you don't have to drive this time of night."

"You don't mind?"

"Not in the least," he said. "I'll pick you up anytime from anywhere."

They sat on the couch in the Florida room looking at the Christmas tree lights Phillip keeps on a bush on the patio. They stay lighted around the clock and remind Phillips of how Louisa loved seeing the multi-colored lights every night during her last years.

"You look gloomy tonight," Phillip said.

"Reading about the wars and rebellions in Jamaica during slavery years is depressing," she said, "and trying to find my ancestor is more difficult than finding that needle in a haystack."

"I know, I had trouble at first," Phillip said. "My paternal ancestors are Bahamians. I finally have solid information on them. One of my great-greats was born at The Crossing on Long Island, Bahamas, in 1783, the year of the mass departure of loyalists from St. Augustine."

"Wow! Is that rock-solid?" she asked.

"Pretty much so," he said. "With the DNA programs available and several Bahamian ancestry groups working to uncover the facts, I learned so much about their lives."

"I wish I could say the same for my Jamaican history. The more I read how horrible it was to live in Jamaica back then as a Black person, the sadder it makes me. Will there ever be a better understanding among all of us who live in a community?"

Phillip did not answer. He wondered the same thing.

Racism and greed are the main causes of anger and violence in the United States. Racism has always been a tool used by malevolent groups. They will use anything to turn people against each other. If the masses are mad at each other, they don't pay attention to what the minority in power is doing for itself and it friends.

The worst of the groups use the color of a person's skin as a reason to separate "us" from "them." White people can never know the depth of racism unless they walk a mile in a Black person's shoes. They cannot fully understand how people of color have to deal with racism every day of their lives in so many ways.

Hatred for Black people in America

may have started when the first African slaves arrived. Where and precisely when that happened is a matter of debate. Some believe that the British brought slaves with them when they landed at Plymouth Rock in 1607. The slave trade in the Caribbean started in 1494 when Columbus discovered Jamaica and led to the genocide of the Tainos tribe. Historians have noted Menendez brought slaves from Spain to St. Augustine in 1565.

Historical documents indicate Britain was more heavily involved in slavery of Black people in the colonies than Spain, which was focused on searching for spices, gold, and silver. Spain wanted to convert indigenous people to the Catholic faith. On the other hand, British colonies wanted slaves to harvest crops and create products for shipment to England. There was an ever-increasing need for more slaves as the British colonies grew and expanded.

Tiana and Phillip talked openly and honestly about racism because they had respect for each other. They knew how evil it was for slavers to kidnap Africans, chain them together, put them in the filthy hold of a sailing ship and feed them barely enough to stay alive. There were slaves from different tribes who spoke different languages all together on British slave ships — floating Towers of Babel.

It is impossible to know the pain experienced by chained men and women when a ship encountered rough seas and they were tossed about the hard wooden decks of the ship. There is a special place in hell for slavers well below Dante's Ninth Circle.

There are still people in America who would enslave people of color if they could. They are people who the better interests of our society must identify, rebuke and watch. The Irish have a blessing for evil people that roughly says, "If you can't turn their hearts or turn their minds, then turn their ankles so they will be recognized when we see them walking down the street."

Tiana and Phillip recognize that white people living in St. Augustine today cannot be blamed for what white people did during the years of slavery. Neither can the Native Americans of today be blamed for the actions of ancestors who slaughtered and scalped thousands of patriots and white settlers.

Tiana and Phillip see the value of discussing the true history of America. Honest discussions could provide closure for people of color. Discussing all of our history is important to ensure that slavery never happens again. We must be awake. That means knowing our past, living in the present and hoping for a better future.

Tiana remembered that St. Ann

Columbus Preparatory Schools won an elocution contest when the topic was: A people without the knowledge of their past history, origin and culture is like a tree without roots. She remembered saying how important that was for all future students.

Tiana said she sometimes experiences racism in St. Augustine in the way people talk to her or look at her. She says there are many subtle ways in which racism can be expressed. For instance, when she goes into a shop at the mall, a clerk usually comes over immediately and asks if she needs any help. She tells the clerk she is just looking and will let the clerk know when she needs help. The clerk leaves, but keeps an eye on her until she leaves the store. Do all clerks think Black people are shoplifters or are clerks simply trained to be more conscious when people of color come into the store?

White people aren't worried about

being harmed or shot if a police officer stops them for speeding or not wearing a seat belt or running a red light. Black drivers know to keep both hands on the steering wheel when pulled over and a sheriff's deputy or police officer approaches the car, particularly if the officer has his hand on his weapon. Black drivers feel they have to be submissive no matter what highway they are on or what city they happen to be in and especially on rural country roads.

Phillip and Tiana believe the only way Black people will ever be treated equally is for communities, big and small, to champion honest discussions between the races and instill in upcoming generations a better understanding of people of color. We are all children of God, Tiana and Phillip often say.

"How can a person hate Black people, or any person of color, and still believe in God?" they wonder.

"Slavery in Jamaica was worse than

it was in St. Augustine," Tiana said. "At one time, 90 percent of the people in Jamaica were slaves. No wonder it takes so long for change to happen."

Chapter Nine

PHILLIP AND TIANA ENJOYED ANOTHER DELEC-
TABLE SHRIMP DINNER AT O'STEEN'S RESTAURANT.
As always, Lonnie's fried shrimp were
perfect, the vegetables were fresh and
the desserts homemade. When they finished, Phillip paid the check in cash and
they walked to his truck. Phillip opened
the door for Tiana and headed west
across the Bridge of Lions to her house.

When they reached the top of the
bridge, Tiana said, "I never get tired of
admiring St. Augustine's skyline or listening to the Cathedral bells."

"Me neither," said Phillip. "I read a
post on the Minorcan Facebook page
that one of the bells might be the oldest in the United States. It was removed
and taken to Cuba when the British controlled St. Augustine and was brought

back in 1784."

"Really," Tiana said. "Well, that is another rabbit hole to go down to see if that if true. Once I get on a rabbit hole site, the next thing I know four hours have passed."

"Roger on that," Phillip said.

They parked in the driveway. Phillip walked Tiana to the door for a good-night hug. As they drew near, they noticed the door was ajar.

"Did you lock the door before we left," he asked.

"I always lock it," she said. "What's going on?"

"Let me go in first," he said.

Phillip opened the door and walked into the dimly lighted living room and flicked on the light. Tiana was standing close to him. Phillip stopped in his tracks when he saw a well-dressed, medium-sized man sitting on the couch with his hands folded in his lap looking straight at Tiana.

"Who are you? What do you want?" Phillip demanded. His muscles tensed.

"Who the fuck are you, old man? What business is it of yours?" the intruder said, rising from the couch and moving toward them.

Phillip stepped forward to the table where a brass candle holder was in reach. He figured the man had a weapon and did not take his eyes off of him.

"What are you doing here, Brantley," Tiana said angrily. "You are the bastard you always were."

Phillip turned and looked at her. He had only heard her use one curse word since they met. Bastard was the word she used then, and she had applied it to Brantley Baxter, who was looking at Phillip through mean, squinty eyes.

"You know why I'm here. I want my documents in the lining of your suitcase," he said.

"I told you I don't know what you are talking about. There were no papers in my suitcase," she said in a loud voice. "Get out of my house before I call the police."

Baxter moved toward them. He was surprised when Phillip picked up the brass candle holder and held it by his side.

"Put that back on the table, old man, or I will stick it up a place where the sun don't shine," Baxter said. Phillip just smiled.

Baxter took two more steps toward them. Phillip feigned a punch to his belly with his left fist, then hit him with the candle holder on the side of the head with enough force to take him down, but not enough to kill him.

Baxter would have nothing else to say until he woke up in the emergency room at Flagler Hospital under the watchful eye of an Officer Critchloe.

Tiana called 911. Phillip removed the knife from Baxter's belt. Baxter groaned slightly, but made no attempt to move or speak. He was out. If he had moved, Phillip was ready to hit him again. There was no way the man on the floor was going to harm Tiana.

Police cars and an EMS vehicle arrived in about five minutes with sirens screaming and red and blue lights flashing so bright it was blinding. Tiana turned the front porch light on and opened the door so they could see everybody in the room. The officers entered the house with guns drawn, but when one of the officers recognized Phillip standing over the perpetrator, they holstered their weapons.

"What's going on, Phillip," Officer Critchloe asked. "Is that the man who broke into the house?"

"Yep," Phillip said. "Glad he didn't have a gun, or this might be a different scene."

Phillip stepped back, put the candle holder back on the table. The EMS crew knelt down beside Baxter to look at the cut on the side of his head and put him on the gurney.

Tiana was shaking, but not bad enough to keep her from putting on water for strong tea. Two of the officers checked the house to make sure all doors and windows were locked. They noticed there was no forced entry at the front door. They put that in their notes. Tiana, Phillip, and Officer Critchloe sat down at the kitchen table. Critchloe asked Tiana to tell him what happened.

"Phillip and I were returning from supper. When we got to the front door, he noticed it was partially open," she said.

"Phillip went in the house first. I was right behind him when we saw Baxter sitting on the couch. Phillip asked him what he was doing in the house. I recognized him immediately and told him to leave the house or I would call 911," she said.

"How did you recognize him?" Critchloe said.

"He is the father of my daughter," she said. Critchloe winced as he made a note in his journal.

"Did you know he was coming to your house? Does he have a key to the front door?" Did he try to attack you?" he asked.

"I did not know he was in St. Augustine; he does not have a key to the door and yes, he lunged toward Phillip," she answered. "He can pick any lock ever made and get into any locked car like he did when he was stealing cars on the island."

"Did you think he was coming after you, Phillip?" Critchloe asked.

"He was coming for me and for Tiana, as well. That's why I stopped him and took his blade away. It's over on the table," Phillip said.

"Was the knife in his hand when he came at you?" Critchloe asked.

"No, but he could have got it with the blink of an eye," Phillip answered.

Critchloe was typing on his laptop as fast as he could, making notes needed for interviews he would conduct later with Phillip and Tiana. He especially needed all the information for the interview with the man on the gurney headed for Flagler Hospital's emergency room.

"OK," Critchloe said. "I have enough for now. I'm going to the hospital. I want to be there when he comes around, assuming he will come around sooner than later. I will see you both tomorrow to finish the paperwork. You good with that, Phillip?" he said.

"Yes. We are good with that. We appreciate your quick response," he said. "I hope Baxter gets to feeling better. Thanks again," Phillip said and walked his friend to the door.

Phillip walked back to the kitchen where Tiana was crying softly. He knew the trauma would prevent Tiana and himself from getting much sleep.

"You want to talk about this now,

or wait until tomorrow?" he asked as he patted her gently on the shoulder.

"When will that bastard be out of my life,? He has dogged me about papers for years. He will not let it go."

"Where is the suitcase he was talking about?" Phillip asked.

"It's in the back of my walk-in closet."

"Will you get it, please?"

She brought out the faded blue Samsonite suitcase she had had for more than 20 years and laid it on the kitchen table.

Phillip opened it, then noticed the aroma of Jo Malone perfume. Louisa's favorite.

"Do you mind if I pull up the lining and see if his papers really are there?" he said.

Tiana was apprehensive. She loved that suitcase. She did not want to ruin it, but she had to find out once and for all if Baxter's papers were in it.

"Okay, I need to know," she said.

Phillip tried to open the liner without cutting it but could not. He drew his Buck knife out of his pocket and cut a small slit across the back of the liner so it would be easy to fix.

He lifted the liner. Sure enough there was a large manila envelope. He handed it to Tiana. She opened it and removed Baxter's papers.

"Oh my god," she exclaimed. "This is a list of Brantley's drug clients and suppliers in Jamaica."

Phillip was stunned.

"No wonder he wanted this," she said. "If the Jamaican drug-interdiction unit gets these documents, all hell will break loose. I have to give it to the St. Augustine police department."

Phillip called Critchloe and told him they had found some documents and asked him to come back and get them. Critchloe was at the house in 15 minutes to pick up the papers.

Chapter Ten

PHILLIP AND TIANA WERE AT THE POLICE STA-
TION ON WEST KING STREET THE NEXT DAY
WAITING FOR THE FINAL INTERVIEW. While
they were sitting in the visitor's room
talking about ancestors, Phillip asked
Tiana about her father.

She told him her father abandoned
her mother before she was born. He
packed up everything he owned and
moved to Turks and Caicos as a charter boat captain.

A longtime friend of her father's had
made a fortune the previous decade.
He bought a hotel and a marina. He
wanted someone to work for him who
knew how to catch billfish and tuna.
More importantly he wanted someone he trusted to captain his 2017
Rybovitch Sportfisherman, equipped

with all the latest bells and whistles.

She did not know if her father's friend had ties to illegal drug dealing, but she was aware that the Turks and Caicos serve as a pathway for narcotics entering the United States from South America. She said her father was never into drug smuggling as far as she knew. He simply wanted to fish every day of the year, if possible.

Tiana told Phillip her mother was living with her parents before she was born and before her father left for Turks and Caicos. It was common for grandparents to raise their grandchildren in Jamaica. Many men run and hide from the responsibilities of raising a family. Tiana's dad would visit her when he came to Jamaica. He would send presents for her with his new wife who cheated Tiana out of gifts that were rightfully hers.

Critchloe came to the waiting area and asked Tiana and Phillip to follow him. There was one other uniformed St. Augustine police officer and two men in suits in the room. The two plainclothes officers were from a federal agency.

After brief introductions, the interview began.

"Ms. Bennett," one of the federal officers said. "You had the documents in your suitcase, so my questions will be for you."

She nodded her head yes.

"From our understanding, Mr. Baxter is the father of your daughter, but moved away while you were pregnant and was not there for her birth. Is that correct?" he said.

"That is correct," Tiana said.

"Did Mr. Baxter ever tell you what was in the documents you retrieved?"

"No, he did not tell me anything about the documents. I did not believe he had hidden them in my suitcase, but he kept saying he did when he called or left messages."

"Do you know what the documents are?"

"It looks like a list of his clients in his drug business."

"Did you recognize any names on the list?"

"No," she replied, "but I only glanced at them for a minute."

They did not ask any more questions. Critchloe had detailed the entire incident in his report.

"What's going to happen now?" Phillip asked.

Critchloe said two things were possible, explaining that Baxter was in St. Augustine on a tourist visa that gave him 180 days to go wherever he wishes in the United States.

"However, if Ms. Bennett or you press charges, we will put him in jail for breaking and entering plus attempted assault. He could post bail and wait for his court date."

The other possibility, Critchloe said,

was termination of Baxter's visa because of his arrest. He would be returned to Jamaica to face their laws. He has not violated any U.S. laws concerning drugs, the officer said, but information in the documents retrieved from the suitcase seemed to indicate that he had violated Jamaican law.

"Our federal agency will send the documents to the Jamaican authorities in Kingston. They will determine Mr. Baxter's situation. He could be charged by the police or the magistrate and make bail. That is up to them."

"He will be a target if he talks about the drug operation to reduce his sentence or if the gang thinks he talked about them to the police," Tiana said.

"Are you going to press charges, Ms. Bennett, or let this play out by revoking his visa and sending him back to Jamaica?" the federal officer asked.

Tiana turned to Phillip and told him she wanted Baxter away from her and

Chandice. Phillip nodded his head supporting her in the decision.

"I don't want to press charges," Tiana said.

"And neither do I," Phillip said.

The officers thanked Phillip and Tiana for their cooperation. Baxter would be left to take his chances in Jamaica.

Tiana and Phillip left the police station and headed back to their jobs. They would have a chance to discuss this episode that evening at Tiana's house enjoying the meal they planned to prepare.

Before they went back to work, Tiana said, "Baxter is in deep trouble and could be targeted for termination."

"Why do you say that?" Phillip asked.

"In Jamaica there is a saying, 'If yuh cyaah ketch Quaco, yuh ketch him shut.' Translated, it means if you can't catch Quako (a bird) you will catch his shirt."

"What does that mean?" Phillip asked.

"It means if the gang is after a man for doing something bad to them and they cannot find him, they will take revenge on his family or friends," she said. "It is still the way things are done in many parts of Jamaica."

Chapter Eleven

PHILLIP AND TIANA WERE SITTING ON THE OVERSIZED WHITE LEATHER COUCH IN HER LIVING ROOM THUMBING THROUGH DOCUMENTS AND TALKING ABOUT ANCESTORS AND THEIR OWN LIVES. They had just finished grilled lamb chops, steamed broccoli and fresh corn on the cob. Tiana had a couple of glasses of Riesling wine.

They discussed the possibility that Tiana's seven-great grandfather may have served as a soldier when Colonel Deveaux's troops recaptured the Bahama Islands from Spain in 1783. The small military operation was not necessary because the Bahamas were returned to Britain under the provisions of the Treaty of Versailles on Sept. 3, 1783. However, it was three or four months before a ship brought news of the treaty to East Florida.

"I was reading the history of Jamaica last night before turning out the light," Phillip said. "There were great people trying to create equality, especially Marcus Aurelius Garvey. What did they teach you about him in school?"

"He was a national hero. Teachers take their students on day trips to see his monument at the Parish Library in St. Ann's Bay," she said. "Does he strike a chord with you?"

"He was larger than life. His ability to organize massive gatherings for the sake of a better life for Black people was similar to Dr. Martin Luther King. But Garvey was different from King in one big way. Garvey wanted to create a Black nation in Africa. He did not want to be assimilated into the white culture of the United States of America."

At one time, Garvey had brought four million people into the Universal Negro Improvement Association as members.

"He viewed the descendants of the slaves who built wealth for their owners as a diaspora," Phillip said. "He said Black people must have their own nation in Africa. He dedicated his life to the pursuit of a place where Black people could create their own economy and governmental infrastructure giving them a way to reach the top of the ladder."

"You know more about Garvey and maybe even Jamaica than I do," Tiana said.

"I'm not sure of that, but his life is fresh on my mind. History that is real gives us facts not taught in any of the schools I know about," he said.

"For instance, J. Edgar Hoover was head of the Federal Bureau of Investigation from 1924 until he died in 1972. He accomplished thousands of important investigations and put hundreds of criminals behind bars that helped keep the nation free," Phillip said.

"We knew who J. Edgar Hoover was in Jamaica," she said. "There were Jamaican officials and activists who claimed Hoover was harassing Garvey because he was Black and had a large following."

"There is more truth than fiction in that observation. Garvey and King supporters complained in the press they were kept under surveillance by Hoover's FBI for no viable reason. That is the reason they are aligned in my mind," he said. "According to an online biography, Hoover's attitude toward King was intense and personal."

That entry reads ...

Hoover used COINTELPRO's operations to conduct his own personal vendettas against political adversaries in the name of national security. Labeling Martin Luther King "the most dangerous Negro in the future of this nation," Hoover ordered around-the-clock surveillance on King, hoping to find evidence of Communist influence or sexual deviance. Using illegal wiretaps and warrantless searches, Hoover gathered a large file of what he considered damning evidence against King. In 1971, COINTELPRO's tactics were revealed to the public, showing that the agency's methods included infiltration, burglaries, illegal wiretaps, planted evidence and false rumors leaked on suspected groups and individuals. Despite the harsh criticism Hoover and the Bureau received, he remained its director until his death on May 2, 1972, at the age of 77.

"I found this comment about Hoover's attack on Garvey," Phillip said.

A full view of Hoover must consider his most egregious attacks. His first prominent target was

Marcus Garvey, a Jamaican man who founded the Universal Negro Improvement Association with the goal of creating a sense of pride and unity among African Americans and the end goal of creating a new independent Black nation in Africa. Hoover was convinced that he posed a threat to the United States and during the first Red Scare in 1919 tried to paint Garvey as a communist to put him in jail. But after sending four agents to infiltrate the UNIA, Hoover came up empty-handed, leading him to pursue Garvey on charges of spying before finally arresting him for mail fraud.

"Reading about what Garvey wanted to do to achieve economic freedom for Black people reminded me of the Tulsa, Oklahoma, massacre on May 31st, 1921," Phillip said. "I wonder if all the hate speech emanating from

Hoover and others against people of color helped ignite one of America's most vicious race riots.

"A thriving, 39-block Black community in Tulsa was burned to the ground because Black people had found economic freedom. Writers believe the massacre occurred because the people were Black and were prospering. Over 300 innocent people were killed. It was one of the nastiest race riots in America and was ignored by historians for eight or nine decades. Not only were Black people killed just for being Black, but the Tulsa City Council passed an ordinance prohibiting the area to be rebuilt causing even more distress. All the people who lived and worked there were forced to relocate," he said.

"How horrible," Tiana said. "I had not heard of that until I saw it on the news last year. I pray nothing like that ever happens again although it is happening in Ukraine and other places where a few evil men control the people. Autocratic tendencies are growing in some of our own states."

"A sad part of current history is so many governors are pressing state legislatures to pass laws forbidding the teaching of real history and are suppressing the vote," Phillip said.

"I guess like most people making their own way in life we don't talk much about our ancestors. We do stand on their shoulders," Tiana said. "I never thought about Garvey very much. I was too busy trying to survive and taking care of myself and Chandice."

"I'm the same way. We have the statue of Pedro Menendez standing on a monument across the street from the Plaza. I rarely look up at it unless I have a visitor who wants to see the sights of our Ancient City. Most of the men who were leaders in forming our nation have statues and monuments scattered all over Washington, D.C., and in towns and cities throughout the country."

"What about the monuments for women leaders in St. Augustine?" Tiana asked.

"Huh," he murmured. "Monuments of women are as rare two Pandas walking down St. George Street holding hands and singing."

Tiana laughed and so did Phillip.

Phillip turned to Tiana and said, "There are millions of good people in America who want to live their lives in peace, happiness, and security. They care about their family, friends and community and know there must be a safety net for the least of the brothers. They work hard every day, they treat people with respect and contribute time and money through their churches, civic clubs and as individuals giving a helping hand."

"I know," Tiana said. "I met wonderful people from Florida while I was living and working in Jamaica. They were friendly and sincere in what they were talking to me about. Meeting them and my desire to earn economic freedom was why I moved to St. Augustine."

"That is a great plan. You are well on your way to achieve the American Dream. So, when you arrived, how did you learn to drive on the right side of the road?"

She laughed.

"I took driving lessons in St. Mary Parish from a man with a big, four-door Toyota. It is a bit crazy and challenging the first time you drive a a car on the island. I don't know if I could have learned in Kingston or a large city. You need a loud horn in Jamaica. When I got to St. Augustine, my uncle's friend had a 2005 Ford Explorer. He taught me how to drive in Florida. He made me drive to Daytona Beach on U.S. 1 and then to Jacksonville on I-95. Yikes."

"What was your favorite place to

drive?" Phillip asked.

"No question about that at all. It was the drive up San Marco Avenue to May Street, then A1A to Mayport. What a great drive even though there is a lot of traffic in Ponte Vedra."

"Did you get a chance to eat at Safe Harbor Seafood?"

"We tried, but the line was out the front door, so we found Singleton's down by the ferry boat and ate there. It was good. The fresh mullet and cheese grits were delicious. And the pecan pie was to die for.."

Tiana moved to steer the conversation in a new direction.

"We spent a lot of time on my ancestors lately," she said. "Tell me about the Bahamian side of your family,"

"My Bahamian roots run deep. They are well documented and getting more so every year with so many descendants providing their DNA reports to a Bahamian historical site," Phillip said.

"I'll tell you about the generations where the data is solid.

"My paternal grandmother was the daughter of a lady who married C. Knowles. He was born on Long Island, Bahamas. He migrated through Key West and went to Tarpon Springs where he met my great-grandmother. Their child came early, and they divorced shortly thereafter. He must have been a terribly busy man. He was married three times and fathered other children. He had eight siblings. He is the person with the most recent and accurate Bahamian history that relates to me and my family.

"His father, my second-great grandfather, was born in 1842 and died in 1926. Eighty-four years means I got great genes. His father, my third-great grandfather, was born in 1809 and died in 1850 at a noticeably early age. I don't know the cause of death. It could have been natural or by accident.

I'm not sure of the source, but I read where one of my ancestors was gored to death by a bull in the Bahamas. His father, my fourth-great grandfather, was born in 1782 and died in 1850, the same year his son died. His father, my fifth-great grandfather was born in 1710 and died in 1765."

"My goodness," Tiana said. "Your ancestors were in the Bahamas in 1783 when my ancestor could have been there for military service as a British soldier. You have so much history to start with. Having that many names and dates are wonderful. Were they all born in the Bahamas?"

"They sure were. I hope I have time to go to Long Island someday and walk on the same island they did. Maybe you can go with me."

"I didn't realize it was so late," Tiana said. "I've kept you up past your bedtime."

"Not at all, but we both have to be

at work in the morning," he said.

Tiana walked him to the door, and they hugged and said goodnight. Phillip got in his truck, turned the radio to XM 70 and headed across the Bridge of Lions to his own bed. His felt joy in his heart.

Chapter Twelve

TIANA AND PHILLIP TRIED TO HAVE SUPPER
TOGETHER THREE OR FOUR EVENINGS A WEEK.
They switched between houses depending on who prepared dinner. Phillip
was a master fry cook. His shrimp,
grouper and mullet were hot, crisp,
and tasty. He knew the best places to
get fresh seafood.

When Phillip was young, he spent
the summer months working near the
water. He and his friends knew how
to catch fish in North River. They had
to catch fish if they wanted to eat
meat. Phillip liked to wade along the
marshes in the fall of the year to catch
fat roe mullet with his 10-foot English
cast net. He told his guests when they
came to his house for a meal, "Fried
seafood without cheese grits is a half a

meal. You will never get half a meal at my house."

Tiana was expert with any kind of dish that included rice. She had learned to put a piece of plastic on the rice pot after the water had evaporated. This little trick steamed the rice and brought out all the flavor. Her oxtails are so tender that the meat falls off the bone. She enhances the taste of the meat and vegetables with garlic, green onions, thyme, black pepper, badia complete seasoning and other Jamaican spices. Irish potatoes, carrots and onions are all musts. She cooks the dish for 45 minutes or an hour depending on the toughness of the meat. There are never any leftovers.

When the kitchen was cleaned and the dishwasher loaded, they sat on the couch in the living room and talked about St. Augustine and Jamaica's similarities. Tiana's progress in finding her ancestor who left St. Augustine to start his new life in Jamaica had been slow going. Phillip loves talking about history. He and Tiana learn something new every time they get together to talk about their ancestors.

"Complete Florida history should be a major part of the curriculum. To deny students a complete education allows ignorance and racism to continue," Phillip said. "Schools should teach the truth based on facts and then encourage the students to do further research from whatever information source they wish."

"Students need to learn the facts without propaganda," Phillip continued. "They should be able to read and study the last wills and testaments where slaves were named and gifted to the descendants the same as giving a horse or a cow or a piece of machinery. Knowing these things does not put blame or shame on any person living today, but these horrible practices must be discussed to prevent slavery from happening again.

"There are thousands of articles describing the slave trade in great detail in books, journals, libraries, and the Internet. Public schools should teach history that demonstrates how Florida got to where it is today, and the price people of color paid with little to show for their efforts."

"Do you think the people are ready for this to be taught in school?" Tiana asked.

"I believe they are," Phillip said. "The information is already out there on the internet and in libraries so efforts to stop teaching the truth will not stand."

"There seems to be too much political rhetoric from government leaders who do not want the real history of Florida taught in public schools," Tiana observed. "One of Sir Winston

Churchill's quotes speaks to the racial division in America: 'A nation that forgets its past has no future.'"

"That's right," he said. "Learning about your history is not about making any one person or people feel guilty — you cannot be guilty of actions that took place centuries before you were born. The question is, why shouldn't high school students learn what actually happened when Florida was formed and how slavery played such an important part in all aspects of Florida's economic foundations?"

"Slaves were captured and brought from Africa by wicked men who sold fellow human beings as a commodity to the American colonists," Tiana said. "Thousands of them were worked to death at plantations and other occupations that needed cheap labor, she said. All those evil men who participated in the slave trade are dead. They were the ones who did the incomprehensible deeds. None of the people living today should be blamed for what their ancestors did."

"But we still have millions of people who do not believe all men and women are created equal," Phillip added. "When 'white privilege' enters a discussion, it is seen as a rallying cry to pull white people down and blame them for slavery. That is not the intent, but can be interpreted as such.

White privilege is a new term. It was coined by Peggy McIntosh in 1988 in her paper, "White Privilege: Unpacking the Invisible Knapsack." Using the word 'privilege' makes it more confrontational than 'white advantage,' blogger Daniel Cubias has said.

There are countless white people who consider themselves far from being privileged when they are working two jobs at minimum wage trying to hold their life together. For them to be called privileged is not the way to start a meaningful conversation about racial injustice. Poor whites suffer economic and social hardship as much as any other group.

"I don't know Jamaica like you do, but there seems to be great advantage for white people in your country," Phillip said. "There is historical inequity because the white descendants of the British colonists own much of the island and most of the wealth."

"You did not have that happen when America won its independence," she said. "The British soldiers and loyalists had a brief time period to leave the country. They could take none of the land. They only could take their slaves to the new place."

"There was a difference in how we removed the British from our land," he said. "It was on our schedule not theirs."

"All of this is history everyone should be able to study," Tiana said. "It was what it was and there is no reason to block true history from students. It seems some Florida politicians want to rewrite history and only teach about things they think should be taught and not what professional teachers know what should be taught."

Chapter Thirteen

TIANA AND PHILLIP WERE ENJOYING THE TAPAS MENU AT THE CASA MONICA HOTEL ON A THURSDAY EVENING. It was a slow night with only 10 other guests. The service was exceptional. Tiana was drinking a rum and coke. Phillip was enjoying a Virgin Mary. He told Tiana it tasted as good as the Bloody Mary he and Louisa used to drink here. They were enjoying a nice meal in St. Augustine's historic hotel. It was so peaceful almost romantic.

"You and Chandice migrated to St. Augustine to join your mother and you worked at your uncle's restaurant on San Marco Avenue, is that right?" Phillip asked.

"Yes, I wanted to go to work the day after I arrived," she said. "I was nervous and excited to be in St. Augustine. Chandice was ready for what was in store for her."

"Did you work at the restaurant until you joined the clerk's office?"

"No," she replied. "I worked at a national retail store adjacent to State Road 16 in the mall for almost three years."

"Why did you leave there?"

Tiana paused. She took a sip from the rum and coke and set the glass down.

"To tell you the truth, Phillip, it was the first time being Black hit me in the face since I came to St. Augustine. It hit me in the heart and hit me in the mind."

"What happened?"

"I liked the people I worked with, but the store manager was unapproachable. That is an attitude some men have when they are managing other people, especially women, and especially a Black woman."

"After two years with outstanding performance reviews and positive interviews with managers in the Fort Worth, Texas, headquarters, I was on the list for a promotion to become assistant store manager."At the same time there were promotions scheduled in logistics and security," she said.

"Six people were being considered, three of them white and three of them Black. When Bill posted the promotions on the bulletin board in the break room, no Black associates were promoted. There was no question that the Black associates were just as qualified based on their performance, but none was promoted, she said."

"What did you do?"

"First of all, I said a half dozen Jamaican curse words under my breath. Then I walked into Bill's office and told him I quit."

He got up and walked around to the

front of his desk to be closer to me. He said, "You don't want to do that, Tiana, you like this job and you are good at it."

"I liked the job and the people, but I said he did not give me the promotion I deserved because I am Black."

Bill denied that skin color had any-thing to do with his decision and Tiana asked him why he had not promoted even one Black employee.

"What did he say?" Phillip asked.

"Nothing. He stood there with the most pathetic look I have ever seen on a man. He had nothing to say. He knew I was speaking the truth. He was still standing in his office when I cleared my desk, waved to my friends, and walked out the door with my head held high."

"Bravo, bravo, bravo for you," Phillip said.

Brantley Baxter was being held in the St. Johns County jail in the custody of the U.S. Customs and Border Patrol office in Jacksonville. As part of the extradition treaty between Florida and Jamaica, the Lapse of Time Article VI says, "Extradition shall not be granted when prosecution of the offense for which extradition has been sought, or enforcement of the penalty for such an offense, has become barred by lapse of time according to the laws in the Requesting State."

Florida law enforcement officers knew the statute of limitations concerning the list of drug dealers and activity had passed, and there was no proof Baxter broke drug laws in Florida. His offense was breaking and entering for which no charges were filed by the victims. None of this mattered because Baxter requested permission to leave for Jamaica during his hearing at federal court. He did not get the documents from Tiana's suitcase and was concerned they would be sent to the Jamaica law enforcement authorities. The existence of the papers might leak to the wrong people. He could be killed.

The Immigration and Customs Enforcement officers transmitted the recovered papers and the St. Augustine police report of the break-in to the Kingston Central police station commanding officer. They also notified them what flight Baxter would be on from Miami.

When Baxter arrived at the Kingston terminal, he spotted two constables standing by the baggage carousel. He looked at them and they looked at him as they approached.

"Mr. Baxter, my name is Officer Johnson" one constable said. "We have a warrant for your arrest concerning drug-related activities." As the handcuffs were being placed on Baxter's wrists, the Constable said, "You have the right to remain silent because anything you say will be taken down in writing and could be used in court."

Baxter was transported to the Kingston Central police station to determine if he could be granted bail there or if a magistrate would be required to make the decision. After a three-hour discussion at the police station, officials decided to hold Baxter and present him to the magistrate the next morning.

Jamaican arrest procedures were similar to Florida's. Baxter was allowed one phone call to let family know about his arrest and detention. He had the right to counsel. If he could not afford counsel, a lawyer would be assigned. The police station is responsible for his safety and food. Safety was Baxter's main concern. If he thought he was being treated unfairly, he could contact the Independent Jamaica Council for Human Rights or the Office of Public

Defender for redress, but that was unlikely. His biggest concern was the possibility that the names on the papers might be leaked. Baxter knew what the gangs would do to his family if they could not find him.

Baxter remembered the press conference the commissioner of police gave in September 2021 when he told the nation the gangsters are "showing a greater willingness to kill family members and associates of their enemies if they are not able to locate their targets." Baxter knew the law of the Jamaican tradition very well, "If you can't catch Quaco, you will catch his shirt." He did not want his sisters and mother killed for something he had done. He would contact his main supplier as soon as he was released.

Chapter Fourteen

TIANA'S RESEARCH CONFIRMED THAT HER SEV-
EN-GREAT GRANDFATHER, WILBERT BENNETT,
JOINED THE BRITISH ARMY. His name was
on a muster roll she found in the archives. He fled the South Carolina
tobacco plantation where he was born
and had lived all his life.

His military training took place in St.
Augustine. He returned to Charleston,
South Carolina as a free man and Black
British soldier. The next time he trav-
elled to St. Augustine, he participated
in a planned incursion to the Bahamas.
After that was concluded and all the
paperwork filed, he was a passenger on
a sailing ship bound for Jamaica to be-
gin the Bennett history that reaches all
the way down to Tiana and Chandice.

Tiana remembered the oral history

passed down by her ancestors beginning with a young Black British soldier
making his way to Jamaica in 1784.
Her grandfather Devon heard the story of Wilbert from his father countless
times and over the years, the story
was passed down to her. Oral history
went from generation to generation before people could read or write. Tiana
trusted it.

Grandfather Wilbert's mother taught
him to read and write. She was a
house servant who escaped working in
the fields. Her mistress taught her how
to read and write, something not common in South Carolina in the 1700s.
She taught Wilbert how to read and
write, giving him a much better chance
in life. Tiana found Wilbert Bennett's
name on a passenger list of a ship that
left St. Augustine for Jamaica in 1784.
She was ecstatic with the find.

Wilbert Bennett was born in South
Carolina in 1763 and died in Jamaica in

1835. His mother was a slave whose parents were captured in Senegambia, Africa. Scholars estimate almost 400,000 enslaved people were sent to the United States during this phase of the Atlantic slave trade. More than one million slaves went to Jamaica.

The British government recognized Wilbert as a free man the moment he joined their army. However, he was not considered free by Gen. George Washington or by the 1783 Peace Treaty. If Patriots captured a Black British soldier, he was still a slave to them and if he was not returned to his original master, he was sold at a slave market.

Wilbert was one of the luckier Black loyalists obtaining passage to Jamaica. He was a free man going to an island where 90 percent of the people were slaves. He was even more blessed by being able to read about world events in the newspapers and periodicals arriving from England. He read about the escalating racial unrest in the British West Indies colonies. He read how slaves were being treated on some of the sugar plantations.

Wilbert arrived three years after the Zong Massacre in 1781. That vile incident was still fresh on everyone's mind. The slave ship *Zong* left Ghana with 442 slaves on board. There were only 208 slaves alive when the *Zong* arrived in Black River, Jamaica.

Crewmen on the *Zong* cast 133 slaves into the sea. Others died of disease, starvation, and malnutrition. When the *Zong* unloaded its "cargo," the captain and crew filed for compensation from the insurance syndicates for the loss of their slaves who were thrown overboard to drown.

A trial was held, not about the murders, but about whether the *Zong* should be paid for the slaves thrown overboard in chains. The captain said the act was done to protect the other slaves, claiming the ship did not have enough water for all the slaves. The jurors ruled in favor of the *Zong*. That court ordered the insurance syndicate to pay 30 pounds for every slave thrown into the sea. Later, an appeals court reversed the decision and ruled in favor of the insurance companies, preventing the slavers from being compensated for killing the slaves.

Neither the captain, Luke Collingwood, nor any crew member was ever charged with murder or any crime. The Zong massacre was the beginning of the end of slavery allowed by the British government. Abolitionists spread this message throughout the British domain.

The British parliament passed the Slave Trade Act of 1788 seven years after the Zong massacre. The act limited the number of slaves that could be transported in a vessel and described how they were to be treated. In 1807 Britain outlawed the trans-Atlantic slave trade and a year later, the United States followed.

The British slave ship *Zong* was originally owned by the Dutch. Its original name was *Zorg*, which means "care." It took 226 years, but on Dec. 28, 2007, Jamaica commemorated the Zong massacre unveiling a plaque at the marketplace in St. Elizabeth Parish.

According to the Trans-Atlantic Slave Trade Database, between 1525 and 1866, the entire history of the slave trade to the New World, 12.5 million Africans were shipped to the Americas. Over 10 million survived the dreaded Middle Passage, disembarking in North America, the Caribbean and South America.

The British government was the biggest participant in slave trading. It is interesting to note that during a trip to Jamaica in 2022, a member of the British royal family did not take advantage of the occasion and apologize for the British slave trade.

Tiana also found "The Book of Negroes," which was compiled in November 1783 and listed Black British army soldiers and Black loyalists eligible for passage from New York to Canada. If your name was not in the book, you could not go.

She found documents telling how American slave owners whose slaves joined the British army wanted their "property" back. The sooner Black loyalists left the United States after the war, the better their chance for survival. One of George Washington's slaves fled his plantation to Canada.

Tiana was ecstatic with her finds. She called Phillip and told him she had something important to show him and asked him to come over. She knew he was leaving early in the morning for a visit with his son Leo in Fort Lauderdale and would not see Phillip for three days. She wanted him to see her findings before he left.

Tiana made chocolate tea and had it ready when Phillip arrived. She gave him a hug, and then they sat at the kitchen table that was covered with the documents she had collected in her research.

"I think I've found what I've been looking for," Tiana said.

"Tell me more," Phillip said.

"There were over 20,000 slaves who joined the British army to gain their freedom. After Britain surrendered, thousands of soldiers and loyalists sailed from Charleston to St. Augustine, East Florida," she said. "My seven-great grandfather, Wilbert Bennett, 1763-1835, must have been among the group from Charleston.

"This is from an article published in London in the *St. James Chronicle* dated Dec. 19, 1782."

From Charles-Town ... brings an account of a fleet having sailed from it for St. Augustine with two regiments of Provincial troops and a vast number of Loyalists.

"Wilbert Bennett must have been on the ship that sailed from Charleston because his name was on a Jamaica-bound ship's logbook in 1784, and he was listed as a Black British soldier," Tiana said.

Wilbert Bennett made friends with two white loyalists during his service as a British soldier, David Bellows and James Stanton. They fought side by side and developed a level of trust that can only be attained under battlefield conditions. Both of them were on the ship with him headed for Jamaica. David's family lived in Jamaica. They had avoided a band of patriots who wanted to kill them and burn down all the structures on their Georgia land. They escaped only hours before the patriots destroyed their property. The family now managed a sugar plantation for a London absentee owner in St. Mary Parish. David offered Wilbert a job at the plantation, and he gratefully accepted.

Wilbert met Amelia Williams the first week after he arrived. Her owner died three years earlier and under the provisions of his Last Will and Testament, she and her family received their freedom. They were young, strong, and attracted to each other.

Amelia was in charge of the plantation living quarters. She was quiet, efficient, and could read and write. She and Wilbert spent every chance they had together. Their marriage is in an annual report submitted to the absentee owners in London.

Wilbert and Amelia were baptized then married by George Liele on the same day. Liele was the first Black Baptist pastor in Jamaica. He was one of the most prominent Baptist pastors of his time. Liele's master was Henry Sharp. Sharp was a deacon in the Savannah, Georgia, Baptist church. He was killed during the American War of Independence.

After Sharp's death, his heirs tried to make Liele a slave again even though he was legally free. British Army Col. Moses Kirkland befriended Liele. He wanted to help him leave the country and avoid being re-enslaved. Liele indentured himself to Kirkland in exchange for Kirkland paying to move Liele and his family to Jamaica.

After two years of arduous work, his debt was paid. He was a free man again. He preached the gospel to slaves, freemen, and a few white people. Liele preached impassioned sermons on the power and forgiveness of the Lord.

The White Jamaican planter class, which wielded strong political power over the House of Assembly, harassed him constantly. They did not want the

Baptist religion to compete with the teachings and beliefs of the Anglican Church. White authorities did not want slaves educated or told anything about congregations having a voice in the function of the church. They did not want Baptist teachings in the Anglican Church. They especially did not want any mention of the "fever for independence" sweeping the Caribbean and other parts of the world. Most of all, they did not tolerate anyone advocating the abolishment of slavery. Greed prevails.

Liele became such a nuisance to the authorities that they declared his sermons and activities seditious. He was arrested, tried, convicted, and led to prison with chains all over him and shackles on his ankles.

He spent three years in a Jamaican prison and was never the same when released. He did not preach any more sermons. He died a quiet death in

1820 at age 70. His legacy lives on. The work he accomplished in the name of Jesus spread to parts of the world hungry for evangelization.

According to a digital collection of records in England, Simon Taylor, an attorney for absentee plantation owners, sent a letter in 1788 to Chaloner Arcedekne, alleging that all the talk about treatment of slaves was incorrect.

I bought for you 7 New Negroes and then 13. I on the 22 bought 33 seasoned ones for Batchelors Hall, they are men, women, and children, been seasoned near the place, and while I am hopeful by and by to establish there a good gang of Negroes, we must have some more. ... As for Cruelty, there is no such thing practised on Estates. I do not believe that the Mad Men at home wish to hurt themselves, but they should endeavour to regulate their own

Police, and show Humanity to their own Poor, before they think of making regulations for our Slaves, who do not wish for their Interference. God knows if they were treated as these Miscreants report, they would have cutt all our throats allready, from what they have allready heard from home.

"That is marvelous Tiana," Phillip said. "Let me read the rest of your discovery."

Her six-great grandfather was Robert Bennett. He was born in Jamaica in 1786, married in 1808 and died at his home in 1856. He and his wife Taniyah had seven children, five boys and two girls. All their names are listed in the baptism records of the St. Mary Baptist Church. Like his father, Robert was a farmer. Also like his father, he and all the family knew how to read and write and were willing to help anyone in the community who wanted to learn. Robert found out early unless a person can discover something new by reading, he cannot have thoughts about what he doesn't know. He was a consummate reader and read classic books found in the rubble of a plantation home destroyed by the rebellion.

Robert was 48 when the British Parliament passed the Slavery Abolition Act in 1833. Slavery in Jamaica was abolished in 1834. Robert lived for 22 years in Jamaica after all people of color were free. With the labor of his family, he provided vegetables to hundreds of freed slaves who found themselves in abject poverty because the sugar plantations shut down and their owners were no longer responsible for feeding or housing them.

There was little work for the 300,000 slaves on the island. The government made few plans to help newly freed people who had nothing start their lives, and they had little chance of finding a job. Millions of Black people starved to death in locations where they were taken by the slavers.

Tiana's five-great grandfather was Marcus Bennett. He was born in Jamaica in 1806. The British Parliament abolished the transatlantic slave trade in 1807 when Marcus was just a year old. Church records show he married Meryl Allen. They had three sons who became gifted farmers before they were teenagers. Marcus died at his home in 1868. His name and birth date are listed in the grave records of the St. Mary Baptist church. He, like his grandfather and father, was a free man and must have celebrated for days with the rest of the country when slavery officially ended.

Her four-great grandfather was Lloyd Bennett. He was born in 1827 and died in 1908. Lloyd had one son;

his wife died in childbirth. Had Delroy not lived, it would have been the end of the direct Bennett line to Tiana.

Marcus and Robert's names are in Lloyd's Holy Bible, which is still in the possession of the family today. Records found in bibles are a trustworthy source of ancestry information. This was quite a find, further verifying the line of Bennetts.

Her three-great-grandfather was Delroy Bennett. He was born in 1860 and died in 1945. There is information on Delroy because he purchased six hectares of land under the Crown Lands Settlement Scheme. Provisions of the scheme allowed small farmers to purchase two hectares and allowed good farmers to buy six hectares. This gave the Bennetts 18 acres of good soil. He and his wife Clara had five sons and four daughters and worked the 18 acres skillfully.

Her great-great grandfather was

Donald Bennett. He was born in 1890 and died in 1980. He was a farmer-trapper and was living when Jamaica became independent. He was the father of three daughters with his first wife and three sons with his second wife.

Her great grandfather was Albert Bennett. He was born in 1925 and died in 2001. He was a farmer/fisherman and father of two sons. Albert taught his son, her grandfather Devon, who was born in 1957, how to fish after a severe drought and a hurricane destroyed the crops on their farm.

Grandfather Devon is still very much alive and close to Tiana. Phillip closes the book on her Jamaican ancestors.

"Wow," Phillip said. "You hit a bonanza."

"I did. I am so excited. I hope you can meet my grandfather someday; you would like him very much."

Historians claim Britain emptied prisons sending the worst of the worst to the Caribbean and the New World. This decision allowed the Crown to save money because they no longer had to house or free these prisoners.

What horrendous lives slaves must have endured if their master was a demented criminal. What unspeakable horrors were done to the slaves by the evil bastards of that era. Slave owners are not normal. How any slave owner could attend church and own another human being is beyond reason. They must believe their god approves of owning people of color. Their god must have been created in their own mind and even likes the same people they like. It's amazing how often that happens all over the world.

"Man's inhumanity to man had no boundary when it came to slaves," Phillip said. "What an everlasting blight on the soul of mankind when men bought and sold people of color as if they were animals instead of part of God's creation."

Phillip and Tiana sat in silence, each deep in their own thoughts. Phillip was the first to speak.

"I'm trying to think of appropriate words describing how unjust the men, women and children of color were treated in St. Augustine and Jamaica during those years. There is still despicable treatment of people of color occurring every day," he said.

"I'm trying to grasp even a small amount of the feelings of a human being snatched from their village, chained to another person on the dark deck of a sailing ship, kept at sea for months with scant food or water then unloaded in a land they had never seen and sold at auction like an animal. I have no words strong enough to define the depth of sin by the slavers or the torment foisted on innocent people because of the color of their skin."

Tiana listened to every word Phillip said. Tears welled up in her eyes. She slid closer to Phillip and rested her head on his shoulder. They sat in silence holding hands for a long time. Tiana looked at Phillip.

"You are a kind man, Phillip Usina. You have a heart filled with love and empathy for people who need help," she said. "But there is no way a white person can ever feel the depth of pain a Black person feels every day no matter how hard they try."

"I hear you," he said. "I hear you."

"Mary T. Lathrap published a poem in 1895," she said. "It speaks wisdom."

Tiana called up "Judge Softly or Walk a Mile in His Moccasins" on her phone and read the last stanza to Phillip in a soft voice.

And remember the lessons of humanity taught to you by your elders.

We will be known forever by the tracks we leave
In other people's lives, our kind-nesses and generosity.
Take the time to walk a mile in his moccasins.

It was getting late. Phillip had to leave early for two nights in Fort Lauderdale.

"Let me know when you arrive safely," Tiana said.

"You bet," he said.

They hugged and Phillip left.

Tiana was at lunch two days later when Phillip called.

"I'm back in St. Augustine," he said. "A day early."

"What are you doing back now? I thought you were staying two nights," Tiana said.

"I had a meltdown after reading the Liturgy of the Hours this morning. There was something strange about the room at the Hilton when I checked in yesterday afternoon. It dawned on me this morning it was the same room Louisa and I stayed in the last time she made this trip with me. I felt like I was suspended in time."

"Oh my goodness. I think it was a spiritual message from Louisa."

"Yes, it was," he said. "Grief overwhelmed me. I could hardly breathe. I had to sit down on the bed. I sobbed."

"I don't know what to say, Phillip. You will grieve for Louisa as long as you live."

"I know. There is nothing anyone can say when I am heartbroken. Waves of grief come when I least expect it."

"Grieving for Louisa brought you back to St. Augustine," Tiana said. "Are you feeling better now?"

"I am. I had to be alone in my car. I want to be in my house. When I'm driving, I contemplate, not the kind of contemplation where you need perfect silence, but the kind that develops after driving over a million miles in our cars during our marriage."

"I understand. Glad you are safely home. Did you spend time with Leo and Katherine."

"Yes. We had a delightful evening. They showed me the large addition they added to their new home on the canal. I had a couple of Virgin Mary cocktails and felt relaxed."

"It sounds like you all had a delightful time. I bet they enjoyed your visit."

"That was the best part. We talked about everything I'm doing and how you and I are tracing our ancestors and enjoying each other's company."

"That's good," she said.

"Glad you are home. I have to get back to work. Talk to you tonight."

"Right," he said with a smile. "Your house or mine tonight."

"Come to mine," she said.

Chapter Fifteen

PHILLIP CAME IN THE FRONT DOOR AND SAW TIANA STANDING AT THE KITCHEN SINK. Her dreadlocks hung down her back. She was still dressed in work clothes — a cream colored, button down and snug-fitting blouse and baby blue jacket pants. Her shoes were off and laying in front of the couch. Phillip stood there for a minute watching her turn the potatoes and onions in the skillet.

"Howdy," he said.

She turned and smiled. She put the knife down and gave him a big hug.

"How are you doing this evening, Phillip?"

"Finer than a frog hair cut eight ways."

"That's mighty fine, Phillip," she said with a laugh.

She had heard him say that line 50 times when she was caring for Louisa.

Phillip hugged her hard and rubbed her dreads with both hands as he always did. She told him dreadlocks have been around more than 2,500 years. He thought dreads started with Bob Marley.

It was Friday. There was no time limit on how late they could work on ancestor history. She served the goat curry from her iron skillet. The hot steamed cabbage was standard. He set a table for two in the dining room. Walking back to the kitchen he told Alexa to play the soundtrack from "How Stella Got Her Groove Back."

Tiana looked at him, shook her head and smiled.

After the delicious Jamaican meal, they enjoyed coffee sitting side by side on the couch in the living room. She knew Phillip wanted to tell her something after his phone call earlier in the afternoon.

"I had an interesting conversation with one of my masonry buddies today," he said. "We were waiting for the crew to finish building the scaffold so we could replace some plaster at the Ponce.

"What did he say?"

"He said, 'Phillip, Roger Smith told me he saw you and a young woman at a restaurant and wondered if I knew anything about her. Roger said she looked awfully young for a date if that's what it was.'"

Phillip was keenly aware of the age difference between him and Tiana. He was aware of an unwritten rule that an older man should never date a woman who is younger than half his age plus seven. In Phillip's case at 75 years old, he should not date a woman under 44. Tiana was 40.

Phillip was a grandfather and could be a great-grandfather soon. Tiana had new horizons, challenges, and opportunities in front of her. Phillip hopes she meets someone her age who respects her and treats her like the lady she is. That is Phillip's most ardent wish. He knew that without mutual respect between partners, chances of happiness are slim.

Phillip's feelings for Tiana were different than any he had ever had. He lost the love of his life a year ago. Louisa was all he ever dreamed of and wanted. That dream came true. Phillip and Louisa's marriage was blessed during all their loving years together.

Phillip's feelings for Tiana came from his respect of who she is, where she is and what she is doing. There would have been no friendship had they not met when she was caring for Louisa with love and affection.

Being in the same house, sitting in the same room, eating at the same table together for over two years created the feelings Phillip and Tiana had for each other. People who see them together at a restaurant or on a trolley train have no idea as to how their relationship evolved. And really, it is none of their business.

Phillip was a senior citizen although one with surprising vim and vigor. Tiana was an attractive young woman. She made him laugh. She brought him joy which he needed. She taught him about her culture. Hugs eased the grief he will always carry for Louisa.

"Well," Phillip said to his mason friend. "She is young, she is attractive, and she is smart. She came into my life when she was assigned to care for Louisa by her employer. She provided nightly care for Louisa during her final years of life. She is helping me in the evenings which is the most challenging time of the day for me."

"I'm sorry Phillip. I didn't mean to pry into your business," he said. "I really didn't."

"That's OK. St. Augustine is a small town. Everybody knows what everybody else is doing, especially all of us who grew up and worked together. I know some things I do make people roll their eyes. That's been me all my life. I'm too old to change now."

Tiana and Phillip sat in silence trying to decide where they were and where they might be going.

"You have feelings about me," he said. "I know you well enough that if you didn't want to be where we are, you wouldn't be. You are one of those strong women I admire who only does what she wants to do. You bring me joy at a time I need it badly," he said. "Are we good with our unique relationship, young lady?"

"We are exceptionally good with our unique relationship. I have never met anyone like you."

"I have never met anyone like you either," he said.

They returned to the kitchen table

to discuss more about Jamaica and St. Augustine.

They began reading documents about slave breeding in the United States to see if it happened in St. Augustine or Jamaica.

They read articles about the increase of slave breeding after the U.S. Congress banned International Slave Trade in 1808. Breeding of physically strong Black men and women took place long before then.

Some historians question whether a slave breeding system ever existed because of a lack of empirical data, but data from the slaves themselves never existed. Slaves were not interviewed during their captivity and had no way to get their case before a court. They felt slave breeding did exist.

Other historians rely on data that is ample plus anecdotal information and interviews with Black descendants of slaves recorded by the Works Progress Administration in the 1930s. Black people interviewed remembered oral history passed down by their parents and friends.

Based on articles Tiana read, Virginia and Maryland were the locations for the major slave breeding operations. The breeding farms operated for the pur-pose of increasing the number of slaves because the farmers could no longer buy slaves.

The situation was much different in Jamaica. Hardships faced by female slaves on sugar plantations stymied the birth rate, and no one has found any records of slave breeding in Jamaica.

Kenneth Morgan wrote a paper, "Slave Women and Reproduction in Jamaica, c. 1776–1834." In it, he not-ed, "Historians have pointed to several reasons for these poor reproductive rates among British West Indian slaves in the final decades of slavery. One line of interpretation emphasizes the poor nutritional state of slaves, heavy infant mortality, strenuous working demands imposed by sugar cultivation, and the brutality of the overseer's whip. Dietary deficiencies in protein and calcium, the high incidence of deaths among infants, the severity of the gang system on plantations, and the underlying discipline imposed by white estate personnel on slaves are essential parts of this explanation. The exact relationship between these factors, however, is recognized as difficult to determine."

Phillip read Tiana an article about a famous sportscaster being fired for talking about slave breeding.

The Washington Post
By George Solomon
Jan. 17, 1988

"Jimmy (the Greek) Snyder, CBS Sports commentator, analyst and

oddsmaker, was fired by the network yesterday after a controversial television interview Friday in which he said many Black people were superior athletes because of breeding from the time of slavery and that the only area in sports left for whites was coaching.

Snyder, 70, had been with CBS Sports for 12 years. In an interview shortly after the midday announcement, he said that CBS executives wanted him to resign, but he refused and was fired by CBS Sports President Neal Pilson in a telephone conversation from Hawaii.

"I told him {Pilson} I wanted to face everyone Sunday," Snyder said. "He told me, 'I can't let you do it.'"

Pilson was not available for comment, but Gene F. Jankowski, president of the CBS Broadcast Group, said, "{Snyder} made a number of remarks about Black and white athletes which had patently racist overtones. CBS wishes to categorically disassociate itself from these remarks."

Snyder's interview with WRC-TV's Ed Hotaling took place at lunchtime Friday in Duke Zeibert's downtown restaurant for a program on the birthday of Martin Luther King Jr. The interview was carried on the 6 p.m. news and picked up by the three networks and other stations.

Snyder's remarks touched off a storm of protests across the country from viewers, television and radio commentators and some Black leaders. He apologized for his statements moments after they were aired and said he did not mean to offend anyone.

A statement by the network yesterday said: "CBS Sports today ended its relationship with Jimmy (the Greek) Snyder. …. In no way do his comments reflect the views of CBS Sports. Mr. Snyder has been a member of the CBS Sports team since 1976 and has made important contributions to its success."

"I remember that incident, but the significance didn't sink in at the time," Phillip said. "You were only 7. I doubt you were reading the sport pages or any newspaper at that time."

"Not hardly," she said. "I don't believe slave breeding was rampant in St. Augustine or Jamaica during those years, if ever."

Brantley Baxter spent the night in the Kingston jail. He was in a cell with one other person. Nothing sinister happened. After breakfast he was taken before the magistrate. The chief constable presented the information noting there was no specific charge that they could hold Baxter on. The magistrate said he did not have to post bail and was free to leave. If they needed to contact him at a later date, they would.

The law-enforcement community in Kingston is small. There are few secrets among those who wear the badge. Whether a law enforcement officer let it be known that Baxter was back in Jamaica nobody knows or would tell if they did know. He could have been seen by somebody near the police station. Nevertheless when Bentley tried to contact his sources nobody would answer the phone. He knew he was in trouble, and his life was in jeopardy.

He thought about hiding in the mountains. He had three places he could hide for a while. He had friends in the hills he had helped hide from trouble. They might reciprocate. He also knew that if the gang was intent on killing him, they had no qualms about killing his friends and family. He did not want his mother and sister killed because he was hiding.

Instead of going to the mountains, he went to Spanish Town where his suppliers were. He hoped he could convince them that none of the men on the list would be charged because there was no evidence of any transactions.

A black sedan with heavily tinted windows pulled up along the sidewalk where he was walking. He looked at the men in the car when the windows were rolled down. He recognized them. Before he could say a word, he took two bullets in his head. He was dead before he fell to the sidewalk.

When her grandfather read about the killing in the newspaper, he called Tiana and told her that for once in Baxter's life, he did the right thing. Baxter's debt was settled. His family was safe. That is the way it is in Jamaica.

Chapter Sixteen

PHILLIP WAS ABOUT TO SAY GOOD NIGHT
WHEN TIANA'S PHONE RANG. She walked
to the table and picked it up. It was
Grandfather Bennett. He never calls
her this time of night.

"Hello Grandpa," Tiana said. "Is everything all right?"

She knew something was wrong and
sat back down on the sofa next to Phillip.

"Hello, Yanique. I am afraid things
are not all right Lovie passed away an
hour ago here at the house. Her big
heart gave out."

Tiana began to cry. Grandpa was
also crying. Phillip held Tiana's hand.

Tiana knew Lovie had been feeling poorly for the past few weeks. Her
brothers visited her at least three times
a week and gave her a report on Lovie's

condition. The doctor told the family there was nothing else to be done. He said, "There comes a time in everyone's life, if they live long enough, their body wears out."

For those who believe in God, dying is the beginning of the next life. Lovie was a true believer and tried to walk the path she believed Jesus wanted her to walk.

"What were her last moments like?" Tiana asked.

"She was beaming. She had the most relaxed look I have ever seen. She looked deep into my eyes, all the way to my soul, squeezed my hands and said, 'I love you,'"

A torrent of tears ran down Tiana's face. Phillip choked up feeling Tiana's sorrow. Neither Tiana nor Grandpa Bennett said anything for an exceedingly long minute.

"What is your plan, Grandpa," she asked.

"We have not made all the arrangements of course, but Pastor Wall is coming over in the morning, and we will make the decisions about the services. She will be laid to rest in the family plot, which you remember is near the tree you climbed on when you were a child."

"Let me know your plans. I will make my plane reservations," she said. "I know you loved her as only a grandfather loves a grandmother. We will miss her dearly the rest of our life."

"Goodnight Yanique. I love you."

"Goodnight Granddaddy. I love you too."

"I want to attend the funeral with you," Phillip said.

"Let us talk about that tomorrow evening if that is all right with you. I have to sort out so many things including getting time off."

"I understand," he said. "That's fine."

She walked Phillip to the door and gave him a hard hug. They said goodnight.

The traditional Jamaican keystone event observed in connection with the passing of Grandmother Bennett was to be "Nine Nights," based on the belief that her soul remains near the body for nine days after death. Her ghost, called "Duppy," becomes a pest to the family if not properly respected. Before Nine Nights begins, there is a religious service at the house. Songs are sung and prayers said to let Grandmother Bennett know it is time to leave.

On the ninth night, her ghost leaves the earth, and the final celebration begins. Music, dancing, testimonies, and memories are given by the family to keep the ghost from coming back to haunt survivors. Grandmother Bennett is mourned by family and all who loved her at the church services. The customary events are grave digging, the funeral, and the wake at the family burial plot.

The grave is dug in the Bennett family plot. Friends help dig the grave. They lay concrete blocks to surround the casket. Grave digging is not solemn. It is an event where food and drink, especially white rum, are served. Members of the community stop by to pay their respects to the family and enjoy the food and drink.

Grandmother Bennett's Thanksgiving Service at the church will be a ceremonial event attended by family, friends, and close acquaintances. The burial will follow immediately at the family plot. There will be a final wake in the yard, which is a key step in the grieving process. Her life will be celebrated as happily as possible. Whether food and drink vendors show up to feed and entertain with music is not known. One writer has suggested that Jamaicans once believed the soul returns to Africa, but today most believe the soul goes to heaven.

The Nine Nights is like other Christian

traditions. The ritual pays homage to the journey of the loved one on earth in preparation for the afterlife.

〰️

Tiana called Phillip during her lunch break.

"What a wonderful boss I have," she said. "He told me to take all the time I needed. If there was anything he needs from me he will call."

"I agree he is a special man. His management style and kindness towards all are the reason he has been unopposed as the clerk of the court for 24 years," he said.

"Are you familiar with the Jamaica customs when a loved one dies," she asked.

"No, I'm not."

"It will take well over a week. We follow a Nine Nights tradition. Grandmother's casket will be at the funeral home. Our friends will sing songs, talk about her, and pray for her each night. The funeral will be at the Church of the Living God followed by burial at the family's cemetery under the trees at the back of the house."

"That is a powerful and beautiful tradition. I want you to teach me all about it when you have time. I can't be away from my job that long, but I will attend the funeral."

"That would be kind of you. I talked to Grandpa about our unique relationship. He would be pleased for you to attend the funeral."

"How good of him. Let me know the date and I will make my reservations. It has been 20 years since Louisa and I visited Jamaica on a cruise ship. I know a lot has changed."

Phillip boarded a flight for a two-night stay at the Jamaica Inn on Main Street in Ochos Rios. It was thirty minutes from Tiana and the Church of the Living God. After breakfast the next morning, he took a taxi to the Bennett home. The veranda was full of people talking and drinking tea. Tiana saw Phillip exit the taxi. She excused herself from the people she was talking to and greeted him on the path. She gave him a hug.

He met Tiana's family and friends milling around on the veranda. Phillip was the only white person at the house. He remembered Tiana being the only Black person at Louisa's reception after the Catholic church services in St. Augustine.

He was apprehensive, not about being white, but not knowing anyone except Tiana. There was no way he would remember all the people he was about to meet. He smiled and nodded to everyone who glanced at him on their way to the back yard where Grandpa Bennet was standing under the shade trees talking to his two sons.

"This is Phillip Usina, my St. Augustine friend I told you about," Tiana said.

"Phillip, this is my grandfather Devon Bennett and my brothers William and James."

Phillip noticed that both brothers applied a lot of pressure with their handshakes. He responded in kind. Phillip had a handshake like a bear. He had worked with his hands all his life. Phillip thought he felt one of the brothers wince a little as they stood there shaking hands and smiling at each other.

"Welcome to my house, Phillip," Devon said. "Tiana tells me you both are trying to find your ancestors. She told me you have ancestors in the Bahamas and from the Isle of Minorca."

Phillip looked at Tiana and smiled. She certainly had told her grandfather everything they were doing.

"Thank you for the invitation. First, please accept my deepest sympathy for the loss of your wife," Phillip said.

"You and I are in the same club," Devon said. "It is a club none of its members care to be in."

Phillip and Devon looked into each other's eyes in a way that only those who have lost their wives understand.

"I love working with Tiana and learning about my ancestors and hers," Phillip said.

Tiana and her grandfather walked back into the house to greet the new arrivals and make sure there was food and drink on the table.

Phillip and Tiana's brothers stayed in the back yard under the shade trees. They looked like they wanted to ask Phillip something.

"What's your intentions with Tiana?" William asked.

"What do you mean, intentions?"

"I mean what do you all have going on. James and I are concerned about her."

"Well, do not be concerned when it comes to us. She and I are dear friends. We became friends when she was caring for my wife while she was dying."

"I did not know that," William said.

"There is a lot you don't know," Phillip said. "Tiana is a special lady. She and I are fond of each other. We grew close under the circumstances we were placed in. I enjoy being with your sister. We talk. We laugh. We reminisce."

The three of them went into the house. The brothers did not have any more questions for Phillip.

Phillip stayed at the house listening to all the stories about Tiana when she was little and lived in the community. After the people left, he called a taxi. Tiana walked him to the street and gave him a hug.

"I'll see you at the church tomorrow afternoon," she said.

"You bet. Goodnight, sweet lady."

Phillip arrived early at the Church of the Living God. He entered and sat in the back row. He was unobtrusive as he read the program for the Thanksgiving Service for the life of Lovie Bennett. It was like the program for Louisa. Full of joyful pictures of the family.

Phillip told his children that when he attends a funeral, like most people, he thinks of his parents and grandparents and all the family and friends who have passed on. He told them he thinks about his own mortality and knows one day his body will be in a casket brought solemnly into the church and then buried in the ground for eternity. He told his children he hoped it would be a while yet before he is called home. He also told them he was no longer afraid of going. They may have appreciated hearing that from their dad.

At 2 p.m., the Bennett family procession into the church began. It stopped at the pew Phillip was sitting in. Tiana asked Phillip to join her. Phillip was confused but stood and Tiana took his arm. He proceeded to the front pew of the church with the family. Phillip sat next to Tiana. He whispered to her that he was proud to be here in this historic church and to be part of a beautiful service for her grandmother. She squeezed his hand.

The opening hymn was "How Great Thou Art," which always brought a tear to Phillip's eye. It was sung at the funeral for Louisa by a church full of friends. There would be no dry eyes today. The second verse reminded Phillip of the years he and Louisa spent at their mountain cabin near Beech Mountain, North Carolina.

"When through the woods and forest glades I wander, and hear the birds sing sweetly in the trees. When I look down from lofty mountain grandeur and hear the brook and feel the gentle breeze."

The singing of the congregation and the choir reached heaven.

The pastor gave a heartfelt prayer

full of thanks to the Lord for Lovie Bennett's long life. William Bennett read Psalm 90: 1-12. The last line says so much, "So teach us to number our days, that we may apply our hearts unto wisdom."

The First lesson was followed by the granddaughter singing a beautiful song. The Second Lesson was read by granddaughter Tiana Bennett reading 1st Corinthians 15: 50-58. The last line offers timeless advice.

"Therefore, my beloved brethren, be ye stedfast, unmoveable, always abounding in the work of the Lord, forasmuch as ye know that your labour is not in vain in the Lord."

Tributes and remembrances from family and friends followed. Kind words of love and affection from those who were loved by Grandmother Bennett were inspiring.

There was laughter and tears throughout the service. Words of affection expressed at the passing of someone you love are powerful. They come from the heart and are spoken only once in the presence of a congregation. The tributes about Lovie's life were like water flowing gently down a stream polishing the rocks. The Offertory Hymn was "When Peace Like a River."

The first stanza touches all.

"When peace, like a river, attendeth my way, When sorrows like sea billows roll; Whatever my lot, Thou has taught me to say, it is well, it is well, with my soul."

Following the hymn, John Bennett delivered a heartfelt eulogy. It was followed by the pastor's sermon stressing the love and power of God and the forgiveness of all sinners who ask and follow His commandments.

He concluded his sermon with prayers for the Bennett family and all who were gathered in the church. He asked the congregation to remember their departed sisters and brothers and pray for them.

The Recessional Hymn was "When We All Get To Heaven," sung with so much gusto it could have been heard in the park across the street. Phillip liked the second stanza: "While we walk the pilgrim pathway, clouds will over-spread the sky; but when trav'ling days are over, not a shadow or a sigh."

Phillip rode in the car with Tiana to the Bennett house. There was little conversation. Everyone was locked in their thoughts and memories knowing they would never hug or touch Lovie again on earth. Phillip held Tiana's hand throughout the long ride to the house.

The graveside service was the Bennett family's last step in letting go. Family and friends from far away plus neighbors in the community watched as the casket was lowered into the ground. There was music in the air and food and drink for everyone.

Tiana squeezed Phillip's hand hard and cried softly when they all sang, "I'll Fly Away." The last stanza is the hope of all people with faith. "Just a few more weary days and then I'll fly away to a land where joys shall never end, I'll fly away."

Phillip stayed at the Bennett home until well after midnight. He was glad he and Tiana had an afternoon flight to St. Augustine.

Chapter Seventeen

AFTER TIANA AND PHILLIP RETURNED TO ST. AUGUSTINE FROM LOVIE BENNETT'S FUNERAL, TIANA NOTICED A SUBTLE CHANGE IN THE WAY THEY TALKED ABOUT LIFE. Phillip knew the significant difference in their ages was an issue he and Tiana had talked about before. Mostly in jest, but true words are often spoken in jest.

They were at Tiana's house and had just finished a great Minorcan supper of chicken pilau, clam chowder and a river shrimp cocktail. Tiana had a glass of Riesling wine while Phillip enjoyed the chocolate coffee she made for him.

Phillip wanted to discuss their relationship; a subject brought up by Tiana's brother William in Jamaica when he asked Phillip about his intentions.

Tiana and Phillip liked each other

and had a special friendship. The years spent learning about each other while taking care of Louisa was the basis for their friendship. It could not have been created in any other way for them. Without Tiana being a caregiver, they would have never met. Without her company in the evenings, Phillip's grief would have been much worse.

They often hugged. That was the extent of their physical contact. Phillip, even at 75 years of age, was still a man. He was with a beautiful young woman. Thoughts of a more intimate relationship crossed his mind occasionally because he was a man and that is where a man's thoughts take him. It was never more than a thought.

Tiana never gave any indication she wanted anything more than the friendship that had evolved over the past few years. There was never any sign she had any desire or intention of laying down with Phillip.

Phillip turned to her as they were sitting on the couch and said, "Do you realize I will be 95 when you're 60. That's something, isn't it," he said.

"I have never given the difference in our ages much thought, Phillip," Tiana said. "Why did you say that?"

"I'm thinking all the time you spend with me you could be spending with someone more your age. You are special. You brought me joy during a tough time in my grieving over the only woman I have ever loved with all my heart and soul."

"Everyone knows you adored Louisa. "She was a lucky woman."

"It's been a year since she died. Without your company, I would have spent so many nights eating a lonely meal. Having you visit and spending these wonderful weeks looking for our ancestors is a godsend."

"What are you trying to say Phillip, are you telling me our relationship is

ROBERT PHILLIP JONES AND VENASA TASHANA WALKER

about to change?"

"I don't know exactly what I'm telling you, Tiana. I just know you need more time with other people, especially your own age."

"I'm not sure you can actually speak about my needs Phillip. I know the difference in our ages. I am into where I am today, not 10 or 20 years from now."

"I understand that. I really do. We learn in AA when you feel confused or worried about tomorrow or yesterday you look down at your feet. When you see your feet, you know that is where you are. I try to live in the moment."

"You are a special man Phillip Usina, and I enjoy your company."

"I enjoy your hugs, young lady, and you know I am a hugger. You are truly a Jamaican lady and I hope your life is filled with joy."

Tiana and Phillip finished a late night snack of milk and carrot cake. Bob Marley's "One Love" was playing as she walked Phillip to the front door hand in hand. He hugged her tightly as he always did. He kissed her forehead, both cheeks and for the first time her open lips. They were wrapped in an embrace for several minutes.

Phillip released his hug. He stepped back and looked into her eyes. They spoke the language of passion. Phillip walked to his truck. Tiana locked the door to her house, then leaned hard against it. She heard Phillip's Ford Raptor pull out of the driveway.

Moments later, she heard the purr of the Raptor back in the driveway. The engine stopped and a truck door opened. She smiled, unlocked the front door, and walked to the master bedroom shower, still listening to 'One Love.' She turned the shower handle to warm.

CPSIA information can be obtained
at www.ICGtesting.com
Printed in the USA
LVHW100643261022
731581LV00004B/176